Finding Doom
T.S.O. Book 1

R.E. Klinzing

To Gracie, an absolutely amazing cousin with an amazing smile. Keep dreaming!

- R.E. Klinzing

Published by Artistic Grace

R.E. Klinzing

Finding Doom

Published by: Artistic Grace

Cover Design by: R.E. Klinzing

ISBN: 978-1-67-038651-9

reklinzing.com

Finding Doom

Chapter 1

The Hospital Room

My head was spinning in every direction. As I opened my eyes bright florescent lights blurred my vision, making the thumping pain behind my pupils worse. The steady sound of beeping filled my ears.

My vision cleared. I was sitting in a hospital bed.

I couldn't piece anything together. Why was I here? My leg began hurting, screaming out to me in pain. My head was still throbbing in a rhythm I couldn't control. *Focus Amelia!*

I stayed as calm as I could, trying not to panic, keeping my breathing at a steady pace. Why was I here, in a hospital? What happened to me? Why was I in so much pain? Did I mess up an assignment? Why couldn't I remember?

I thought back to a conversation I had with Ms. Blanchard when I was first recruited for the Teen Spy Organization. I can still hear her stern voice from my first day on the job. Her dark hazel eyes were watching me, aware of my every move. "We are part of the T.S.O., the Teen Spy Organization. We take our work very seriously."

"I don't know what to say," I said to Ms. Blanchard. "What will my family think? What about school? Do you really think I can do this?"

"I wouldn't have talked to you about recruitment if I didn't think you were able to do the job. We only look for the best here."

All of it was coming back to me. Her voice was ringing in my ears. "We take our work very seriously." I saw her arms folded firmly in front of her, covered by her navy-blue suit sleeves.

The memory faded. I kept my eyes closed, trying to piece together my thoughts.

"Hey Honey," a gentle voice said, pulling me away from the memory. A gentle hand stroked my hair. I twisted my head around to face where the words came from. Mom sat beside the bed, her blue eyes smiling at me.

"What happened?" I lifted my head to look around the hospital room. My head throbbed like something was pushing me back down onto the pillow, but I ignored it. Dad stood next to Mom. They both smiled at me, clearly relieved I was awake, but neither of them answered my question. A girl got up from a chair and made her way towards me. Her blond hair, covered just past her shoulders, swayed to the side as she leaned down and hugged me. Something about her didn't feel right.

"Hey," she said, pulling herself off of me. I knew who she was, but it took me a moment to put a name to the face. Emily, my best friend. I felt bad, not immediately recognizing who she was. Emily and I have been friends for years, at least it felt like it. Not a single memory about her came to mind.

As I looked past her, I spotted one other person in the room. Ms. Blanchard stood against the wall; hands folded in a professional posture in front of her. A slight look of relief spread across her face as I looked at her, but it hardly lasted a second before returning to its usual stern and expressionless gaze.

Why was Ms. Blanchard here? I was about to ask, but I thought of all the other people in the room who didn't know who Ms. Blanchard really was to me. It was better to play it safe, to save the important questions for later.

"How long was I out?" I asked. The thumping pain in my head started to calm down. I pulled myself into a complete sitting position, using my arms to push myself up. I peered down at the bed. My right leg was propped up on a pile of pillows, covered in a white bandage all the way up to my knee. I didn't let my thoughts focus on my body, knowing it would only make the pain worse.

"You were out for two days," a new voice said. The doctor stood just inside the door. I didn't see him come in. "Hello, Ms. Zegro," he said, smiling at me. "You've got a pretty bad head injury and a fractured knee." He glanced at his clipboard before continuing to speak. "I'm just going to talk to your parents for a moment."

His white coat stood out against his dark skin and black hair. My parents made their way to the other side of the room and the doctor began to speak in a hushed voice.

I brought my hand up to my head, wincing at the

9

pain from the pressure of my fingers. There was a bandage across the side of my forehead and a few scratches on the side of my cheek.

A fractured knee. No big deal. An injury like that would heal overtime.

It was the head injury the doctor spoke of that I was worried about. If an agent couldn't think straight, how could he do his job? I have to be in working order. If not, then what am I good for? What type of head injury was the doctor talking about?

I didn't pay much attention as the doctor spoke to my parents. Ms. Blanchard never left her spot on the wall. Her hands were still folded in their superior way and her eyes were fixed on mine. Something about her expression left me feeling ashamed. Why did she look so unhappy with me? I quickly looked away from her.

"She's going to be a little disoriented," I heard the doctor say to my parents. "Complicated situation." I only heard bits and pieces of what he told them. "Partial memory loss." "Possible black outs" "It's going to take some time."

What did he mean memory loss? I took a deep breath, trying to remain calm even though I had no idea what was happening.

What exactly was I not remembering? My name is Amelia Zegro. Check. How old am I? Fifteen. What grade am I in? I'm a freshman at Glayfield high. I work for the T.S.O. Check.

I looked at Emily and her wrinkled brow, filled with concern. She smiled at me from the edge of the bed. What on earth is going on? I still knew who I was. But I didn't know who she was. Emily looked like a stranger to me. My mind was still trying to process who exactly she was, and why I couldn't remember her.

Two days later I was on my way home. There was no longer a bandage on my forehead, but all the scratches were still there. I hobbled inside the house on my crutches, still getting used to leaning on them for support. It wasn't often I had to rely on someone, or something else, to get by.

"Why was Ms. Blanchard there?" I asked Mom as I sat on the couch. I finally felt comfortable talking about what happened. It was all so confusing.

"Well," Dad started, "as your homeroom teacher she wanted to check on you." *My homeroom teacher? When did that happen?* At that point I thought it was probably a good idea not to reveal Ms. Blanchard's true identity: my controller, my boss, and the head of T.S.O.

"We're just glad you're back home safely," Mom said, sitting next to me. "You scared us. That car could have done so much worse."

A car accident? They had no idea what had really happened. Come to think of it, I could barely remember myself. I knew the car was a cover-up story. It had to be. I would never have let a simple car accident put me in the hospital. It seemed far too convenient. I looked down at the bandage on my leg, wondering what really happened. It was as if my thoughts were drowning in an empty swimming pool. Even though it was empty, nothing holding me down, I couldn't get up.

If my parents didn't know the true story, and I didn't know what happened, who was going to tell me? Ms. Blanchard might know. She might have been there to make sure I didn't say anything about the T.S.O. in my sleep. Sometimes she can worry too much. "We only look for the best here," she said to me. It was two years ago when I was first recruited for the T.S.O. Am I not able to take care of myself by now?

I gave my parents a week smile. "We're just glad you're home," Dad said.

I pushed the thoughts of the accident out of my mind, knowing worrying wouldn't bring me any answers.

Chapter 2
Tony

A few days later, with the help of some crutches and my best friends, Emily and Tony, I was back at school. Unlike Emily, Tony felt familiar to me. I knew him and remembered him when I saw him.

I headed to my homeroom class. Everyone was asking how I was, glad I was back. I smiled at them, wanting them to stop talking.

So, Ms. Blanchard being my homeroom teacher was just another lie too. The same teacher I have had all year was still here. It was just something said to keep my parents happy and out of the dark. Ms. Blanchard wasn't anywhere near my school.

The day went by like any other school day. Once lunch came along, I met Emily and Tony at the lunch tables looking over the soccer field.

"You had me worried, Amelia," Tony said. It was the first time I had seen him after the accident. He combed his hand through his black hair. "That looks like it hurt." Tony looked down at my leg. The three of us sat at benches outside the school, looking over the soccer field. Our lunch period was almost over.

"It's not as bad as it looks," I responded with a smile. The pain didn't bother me anymore. I had gotten used to it.

I looked over at Emily, wondering if she knew anything about the accident. I didn't know why she would, but it was worth a shot. Something told me to ask her. Ever since I saw her at the hospital, I felt like I didn't know her. Her face felt foreign to me. The fact that she knew who I was made my stomach turn. I wanted to know her, I had to have known her, but my head hurt just thinking about how strange she felt.

I looked around me at the busy high school. Kids walked in and out of buildings and others sat at lunch. But no one was paying attention to me and my group.

"Emily," I started, looking over at her. She smiled at me. "Do you know anything about the accident?" I asked, trying to sound innocent. "I can't remember what exactly happened. Do you know what the doctor said or anything?"

Emily looked at me with a gentle smile. "I'm sorry," Emily said. "I don't. I got a call from your dad saying you were in the hospital, asking if I could come over. He said you were in a car accident, a hit and run driver."

"Sounds scary," Tony said from across the bench. A feeling of disappointment washed over me. For some reason I felt like Emily would have known something, that she would have more information. I guess I was wrong.

"Hey, do you remember that time we were riding to

14

the park and saw two cars collide on the other side of the street?" Emily asked.

"I remember!" Tony said. "That was a wild day."

"Yeah," I said, feeling like that was the right response. I tried to picture it in my mind, but I couldn't. "No," I said, changing my answer. "I can't remember." As I said this Emily changed from a bright smile to a look of disappointment.

"That's alright," Tony said, roughly nudging my shoulder. I couldn't sit here anymore.

"Well," I looked at my watch, "I've got to get going. I'll see you guys later," I knew Emily and Tony were watching me as I got up and walked away on my crutches. It probably seemed odd, me just leaving in the middle of our conversation, but I couldn't come up with a logical reason why I was leaving. I didn't even know why I was leaving, but I knew I couldn't sit there anymore. I couldn't get my thoughts to focus.

Chapter 3

Reassigned

For the next month my world continued to feel slow and pointless. I graduated from crutches to a brace. And the relief of not relying on my crutches to walk around was overflowing.

Thankfully, I was still able to participate in choir, my brace not preventing me from singing. My mind still felt empty, a void that couldn't be filled.

I finally worked up the nerve to talk serious business with Ms. Blanchard again. The look she gave me at the hospital was *not* welcoming. What was she thinking about me? Had I somehow let her down? I had been away from the organization for way too long.

It was time to make the trip into headquarters.

The city bus dropped me off just down the street from my house as usual. As the bus turned the corner, I watched it drive out of sight, as I stood alone on the sidewalk. My heart raced. I had been waiting to go back into headquarters and now was my chance.

I crossed the street in the opposite direction of my house and walked three blocks into the city. I made decent time considering the brace on my knee.

I limped across the street, trying to not draw any attention to myself, and stopped on the corner. I glanced behind me to see if anyone was following me. No one was there. Why was I feeling so paranoid? Just calm down.

There were a few cars driving through the intersection, while others waited at the light. Just a few random pedestrians walking mindlessly down the street. Everyone appeared to be completely unaware that the most secretive spy organization in the country was thriving just beneath their feet. The thought of returning to headquarters made my stomach turn with excitement. I couldn't remember the last time I was here.

I looked behind me. No one was paying attention to me. "Ugh, stupid brace," I muttered to myself as I tried to dart into the alley. Even with all my training at the T.S.O. a simple brace was preventing me from running. I leaned over in pain. My knee ached, throbbing like it did in the hospital. I forgot I couldn't run yet. "I can't wait to get this off." After rubbing my knee for a moment, allowing the pain to disappear, I looked up into the alley.

On my right was a tall abandoned parking structure with cement walls. Near the center of the alley a red brick wall stuck out creating a space where the trash dumpsters used to be. The space behind the wall was hidden from the street on both sides. On the opposite side was an old thrift store. Hardly anyone shopped there, so not many people travel by the alley. The other end was blocked off by another cement wall.

Hidden behind the brick wall, I held my hand up to the third brick from the corner where the brick wall attached to the parking structure. A quiet beep told me the hand scanner hidden within the wall was validating my hand print. I stepped onto a square shaped slab of concrete just near the hidden scanner. The concrete slab quickly lowered into the ground with a quiet whoosh. Before I had time to think about it, another slab of concrete slid into its place overhead. The inside of the elevator was dark, but I could still see. Down it went, to the entrance of the T.S.O. headquarters.

Forty feet down, the tube-like elevator landed in the corner of a small office. The silver, shiny walls appeared to be a combination of metal and rock. It was a drab room with a small couch and two chairs against the wall. There was a small coffee table with magazines and newspapers from all over the country, and a water cooler against the wall to the right, just next to a closed door. That was the stairwell door, an emergency exit leading to another part of the parking structure four stories above. The receptionist desk sat near the opposite wall. Directly across the room was the double door entrance to the World Headquarters, of the Teen Spy Organization.

I crossed the small room towards the double doors, smiling with excitement. The receptionist, a nice grandmotherly looking type of woman, looked up at me past her reading glasses. "Welcome back Agent Z," the woman said.

I smiled and greeted her as I continued into the main office. Just as I walked towards the double door entrance, the doors slid into the walls and out of sight, not making a sound.

"Agent Z," a young woman said as I walked past her. "Welcome back." Two more people welcomed me again as

18

I made my way to Ms. Blanchard's office. It was wonderful to be back! Words couldn't describe how fantastic it felt. With a smile on my face and butterflies in my stomach, I headed down the halls.

My world was no longer pointless. I was home, ready to do my job; ready to make the world a better place, one case at a time.

I found Ms. Blanchard in her office, a neat stack of files beside her on the desk. I had forgotten how clean it smelled and how organized it always was. I was surprised by the warm welcome she gave me.

"Welcome back Agent Z. It's good to have you at work again." Ms. Blanchard looked up from her pile of reports and walked around her desk. I shook her hand, remembering her firm grip in mine as she smiled warmly at me. Her dark brown hair, curled professionally, draped over her shoulders.

"Thank you, Ms. Blanchard. It's good to be back." I smiled at her, pushing the excitement down, wanting to look professional in front of my boss. Ms. Blanchard was in charge of everybody. She was the head of the board for the entire organization. Every base in the country, every single mission had to go through her verification first.

"I don't know if you heard yet, but the suspect you were after has been caught," Ms. Blanchard said, walking back to her desk. "As the police showed up, they saw the suspect's car getting away and chased after it. They later found the car in a parking lot with the suspect still inside," Ms. Blanchard assured me. Her dark brown eyes looked at me as if waiting for me to disagree with her.

"So, what about the story of the accident?" I asked, ignoring her criticizing gaze. She still hadn't told me what had happened, or who it really was.

"Don't worry. Everything has been taken care of. Our connections with the police have put the cover story out," Ms. Blanchard reassured. I had no idea what connection she was talking about. I wanted her to tell me something, anything about the accident in detail, like, who put me in the hospital? But I didn't interrupt her. There was no way I was going to question her authority. I let out a deep breath and nodded my head. The boss was always right. Ms. Blanchard continued. "I have a new case for you."

A new case? That was surprising. I thought she would have wanted me to completely heal before giving me a new assignment. I knew she was trying to change the subject, but I went along with it.

"My brace hasn't come off yet. As much as I want it, I don't know if I'm ready to get back in the field yet," I responded.

All I wanted was a new case to take things off my mind, not that there was much in my mind to distract me from. I still couldn't remember certain things, that was the scariest part. It was the not remembering that bothered me.

"No one else can get as close to Savannah as you can. You know her the best in this organization and she trusts you."

"Savannah Bakers? My classmate?"

At least now the name of the organization is making more sense to me. When I first came to work for the T.S.O., it was because they said I had what it takes. They recruited teens for the job, said we would never be suspected. They trained us at a summer camp, then we were assigned our first mission and trained on a more advanced level at the headquarters, that is, if we made it that far. I didn't think I would be spying on other teenagers; especially my classmates.

"I don't see what Savannah could possibly be involved in, or why she is a suspect of the T.S.O."

Ms. Blanchard laid it out. "Savannah is one of the most recognized and gifted young scientists in the state. I presume you already know that. Three years ago, her father, Robert Bakers, was put in jail for stealing secret government documents related to a top-secret military weapon. We have reason to believe that Savannah may be planning on helping her father escape. We don't want that to happen. We don't know what she is planning, how she's planning it, or who else might be involved. Your job is to find out and prevent it from happening. Are you up for the task Agent Z?"

I hadn't known Savannah's dad, Mr. Bakers, was in jail. Truth be told, I didn't know very much about Savannah at all, only that she was smart, and she was shy.

"You can count on me Ms. Blanchard," I said, wondering how much of a challenge this was going to be, how much trouble Savannah could have gotten herself into.

Chapter 4

The Prank of the Year

For the next two weeks I tried to get close to Savannah. With all my effort, I didn't seem to be making any progress. I was never really close to Savannah, just a simple friend, another girl in her class. She never talked to anyone on a sentimental or personal level, not that I knew of.

"Hey Zegro," Tony said coming up behind me. He has a habit of calling me by my last name. "Heard you're getting your brace off tomorrow, must be exciting."

"Definitely!" I couldn't wait to get my brace off. "You ready for your prank on Emily?" I asked, recalling his latest endeavor to mess with Emily's head. "You remember, right? You were going to mess with her computer, make her think someone hacked it."

This was going to be "the prank of the year" as Tony would say.

"I wonder what her face will look like," Tony said as his voice shot up in pitch and he balled his fists. "I've got to get to class. See you later." With that he turned and began walking away from me.

"I just hope it isn't too serious!" I shouted, cupping my hands around my mouth to make my words louder as he walked away, trying to warn him to keep everything under control this time.

His last attempt at pranking Emily ended with her desk full of whipped cream and weekend detention for him. Even though Tony always let me in on his little pranks, I never got punished.

The next day, as I headed to choir practice, I heard Emily shout in the hall. "Why would you do that? You scared me. I thought I erased my homework! My mom's computer was hacked yesterday." Emily sounded very upset, and hearing about her mom being hacked was new information to me.

"Sorry Emily," Tony replied, muffling a laugh. "I thought it would be funny. Amelia and I got a kick out of it."

I walked up behind Emily, tapped her on the right shoulder and waited for her to jump. I needed to know what she was talking about. She did just as I expected. With a little shriek, she turned around, laughed, and then said to me, "Were you in on this?"

Ignoring her question, I went straight to the point. "Whose computers were hacked?" I asked, making sure I heard her properly before I made any assumptions.

"My mom's computer. I don't know who did it," she responded, looking crossly at Tony. Why would Emily know who it was? I thought of Emily's mom. Mrs. Steinfeld was the chief of police. It didn't seem like just a coincidence.

23

"Hey, at least I didn't get caught this time," Tony said, seeming very proud of himself.

"Oh, just you wait," Emily responded, but I wasn't paying attention anymore.

All I could think of was the fact that Mrs. Steinfeld was the chief of police. She had information about dangerous people, about important situations.

I turned and headed to choir. And to my surprise Savannah showed up.

She'd never been in choir before. Why would anyone join a class this close to the end of the school year?

I took a seat towards the back of the room, appreciating not having to wear the brace anymore. I rubbed my leg, stretching it out in front of me.

As practice began, I thought about Savannah, wondering if there was anything that could give me some information on how to get close to her.

Wait, Savannah's birthday is this weekend. She usually invited the entire class to a birthday party or had a girls' sleepover. Last year, she wouldn't let anyone in the back room of the house, not that anyone asked. But I was going to have to get back there. Somehow.

Chapter 5

The Sleepover

Just as I predicted, Savannah hosted a girls' sleepover at her house. She gave out her invitations with late notice, but I didn't care. I would be able to get into her house. Where any secrets might be kept.

Going to Savannah's this time was going to be very different. I was the only one at the party who knew why her dad truly wasn't there. I couldn't wait to get into the mysterious room at the end of the hallway.

While making our own pizzas we listened to Savannah's favorite songs. I wasn't interested in the music she was playing. I was more focused on making sure my pizza was covered in cheese and pineapples. After all, this was still a party.

Emily snuck up from behind and covered me in flour. "Hey!" I exclaimed, turning around to face her. Smiling, I splattered tomato sauce in her face and everyone stopped to look at us. Emily started to laugh, then everyone else joined in. The party continued, and everyone enjoyed themselves, but I couldn't let myself go into full on party mode, not since I was here for more than just birthday activities.

As the pizza cooked, Emily washed her face and I rinsed out my hair in the shower. Everyone went to set out their sleeping bags in the T.V. area. Emily had already joined everyone in the living room. Unwrapping the towel from my hair, I opened the bathroom door. Savannah walked into the kitchen across the hall. With the towel still in my hand I tiptoed across the hallway and peeked inside the kitchen.

"He said to leave it in here for him," Savannah whispered under her breath. I listened carefully, staying as quiet as I could. I leaned against the wall, just out of sight.

Savannah took a small object from her pocket, opened a drawer near the fridge and placed it inside. I couldn't see what it was she was holding, but it had to be important.

I held my breath. This could be what I was waiting for. My heart started racing. I always loved the mystery that came with working at the T.S.O.

As she closed the drawer I darted back into the bathroom and hung the towel up, sighing with relief that Savannah didn't see me. I put a smile on my face, wondering what Savannah meant, what she put inside the drawer. The smile didn't leave my face as I left the bathroom.

While eating our pizza, we watched a movie. One of Savannah's cousins constantly imitated the show, making it difficult for everyone to stop laughing. Once the movie was over and the pizza had been devoured, we made delicious ice cream sundaes. I covered my ice cream in M&Ms and chocolate syrup. We all sat down in a circle in the living room and began a game of truth or dare. I knew exactly what I wanted to ask Savannah, but I was afraid I would give something away. Either I'd get the answers I need and possibly blow my cover, or I wouldn't find anything out at all.

It was Emily's turn. "Okay, Savannah truth or dare."

"Truth," Savannah stated confidently.

"What's in the back room?" Emily questioned, surprising me. My eyes became wide and I held my breath. Everyone became quiet.

"What do you mean?" Savannah asked. Her smile disappeared.

"The door is always locked," Emily said. I thought Savannah might begin to cry. She started folding and unfolding her hands in her lap and couldn't keep her eyes on anyone.

"It's just storage," Savannah replied. I knew she was lying. She couldn't sit still.

"Okay," Emily said with a shrug of her shoulder. The game continued and Savannah became noticeably comfortable again. Watching Emily, I noticed how intently Emily seemed to be focusing on Savannah's every move. When she caught me looking at her, I turned away. Both of them had to be hiding something. I could feel it.

When our ice cream was finished Savannah picked another movie and everyone started to fall asleep. Everyone except me.

Chapter 6

Pink Key

When I was sure that everyone was asleep, I got up from my sleeping bag and walked into the kitchen, hoping to find whatever Savannah put in the kitchen drawer earlier. This was my chance to look around. I turned the corner and walked into the kitchen, but the lights were already on. I slowly walked in, heart pounding. Why would someone else be up?

I saw Emily digging through the drawer next to the refrigerator.

"What are you doing in here?" I asked, a little upset now. At least it was just Emily, but my chances of finding whatever it was Savannah put in here had become slimmer by the second. I must have missed Emily leaving the other room. Or I actually fell asleep.

"What are you doing here?" She asked me back.

"I'm just getting a midnight snack, why are you looking through the drawers?" The look on her face told me that she wasn't going to reveal anything. Emily was a blank slate, only a simple smile meeting me back.

I was bummed my cover was almost blown, and Emily didn't look too happy either. "I couldn't find the silverware," Emily whispered to me. "And you're the one with the memory problem," she joked.

As she said this my heart sank. I still couldn't remember what happened to me. I pushed the thought of my unknown accident to the back of my mind and walked over to where Emily was standing, next to the fridge with an opened drawer. The moment I started walking towards her she closed the drawer. Without saying anything I walked past her and opened a drawer on the opposite side of the counter. "Thanks," Emily said, walking over and taking out a fork.

After eating a scoop of ice cream, we went back to the T.V. room. I lay down wide awake, wondering why Emily was really in the kitchen. She was my best friend, I always know when she's lying and something wasn't right.

An hour later, I decided to get back up and try again. Maybe Emily found something in the kitchen before I stopped her.

I went back to the third drawer next to the fridge. The first thing I saw was a tray full of keys. Maybe that's what Savannah had put in here, a key.

I dug through the drawer, trying to find something that stood out to me, something Savannah would use or even hide. In the back of the drawer, I found a pink key. It wasn't in the tray with the others, but hidden behind a small recipe book inside the drawer. That had to be it.

I picked up the pink key, admiring the simplicity of it in my hands. Smiling down at it, I knew I found what I was looking for.

"Amelia, what are you doing?" Emily whispered from the kitchen doorway. I turned around, grasping the key in my hand. So, she wasn't asleep, and now my cover was blown.

"I thought you were asleep," I said. "What are you doing in here?" She didn't answer. She gave me a concerned look, her eyebrows scrunched together as she waited for me to say something else. I looked down at my closed fist, holding what might be the answer I've been waiting for.

"I wanted to see what was in that backroom. Your questions made me curious."

"Alright then." Emily shrugged her shoulders. "Let's go."

"Seriously?" I asked, loosening my grip on the key.

"Yeah." Emily motioned towards the kitchen's exit. I walked down the hallway with Emily, wondering why she was so willing to do this with me.

Finding the door was difficult since the hallway was so dark. We walked slowly, my hand out in front of me for balance. I held my breath and walked as lightly as I could, hardly hearing the pitter-patter of our feet on the carpet.

Emily and I stopped at the doorway. I looked at her, she looked at me. Emily nodded her head at me, reassuring me it was okay. Taking a deep breath, I inserted the key. Turning the metal object in my hand, I heard it click. I could hear my heart beat as it pounded in my chest, my blood racing through my veins. With my knuckles gripped over the knob, I opened the door.

Chapter 7

The Back Room

With not a single noise, the door swung open. "She must come in here a lot," Emily whispered. A small light went on. Thin red beams of light crisscrossed around the room. "This must be a pretty important storage room if she needs laser beams in here."

"I don't think it's a storage room, Emily," I replied even though she probably figured that out. I didn't know what I expected to find. Emily stared intently at the wall just left of the doorway. I couldn't see what she was looking at. Aside from the light emitted off the laser beams, it was as black as the depths of the sea.

From what I could tell, the room was larger than I expected. Along the walls of the room, where the light from the laser beams let me see around them were the outlines of unusual machines and devices.

Without thinking twice about it, I stepped closer to

the first beam. There had to be a way to turn these things off, to see what secrets were held inside these walls. My best chance of finding any evidence Savannah was going to break her dad out of jail was probably in here.

With my heart pounding inside my chest, I hopped over one of the laser beams, slowly sliding on my stomach under the next. Thoughts of training at the T.S.O. filled my mind as I thought about my next move. I went through many drills just like this. Rolling onto my back my knee began throbbing. I'd forgotten about my injury. With a slight groan, I pushed myself across the floor, wondering how to face the next beam without hurting myself.

I pulled myself into a crouching position, ready to step over another beam without touching the one above my head.

Then the lasers disappeared. I blinked, unsure what to think as I placed my foot back on the floor. A small desk light came on a few feet in front of me. Emily began to laugh. "There was an off switch on the wall," she pointed out, smiling at me as she spoke, as if I should have realized the switch was there. I nodded my head at her, letting out a small laugh.

In my opinion an off switch on the wall wasn't exactly the smartest idea. There wasn't even a keypad to turn them off. At least it made it easier for us.

I stood up and took in my surroundings from the middle of the room.

There was a 3D printer placed on top of a large filing cabinet and a well-organized welding station. Up against the wall at the back of the room was a desk with drawers. Papers were stacked neatly in a pile at the side of the desk. There was a cup holding a few writing utensils. On the middle of the desk was a laptop and the desk light, now dimly lit, was facing the screen.

"Quick, duck!" I heard Emily whisper through the air. She closed the door and turned off the lights. I crouched behind the filing cabinet, once again thrown into the sea of darkness.

The door slowly opened and in walked Savannah.

Within the darkness of the room it was difficult to make out her features. She seemed so fragile, only a little bit of light illuminating her features from down the hallway.

"Is anybody here?" she stammered. I found it hard to believe that Savannah, a quiet, calm, shy person could do anything that could remotely be considered illegal.

"I thought I heard something," Savannah said to herself. "He can't know I left the door unlocked during a party."

Reactivating the laser system, Savannah turned and shut the door behind her. I waited till I heard the lock click and the sound of her footsteps quieted. She had another key somewhere. The one we took was for someone else. Who was the "he" she was talking about? I hoped she didn't notice the empty sleeping bags in the living room.

Emily was still standing by the light switch and turned the system back off. Then the desk light flickered back on.

"That was close," Emily whispered through the dimly lit room. I stood up and looked around, listening to the humming sound that some of the odd machines were making.

Turning my attention back toward the desk, I opened the laptop.

The screen flickered on, showing a picture of the

sunset. In the middle of the screen was a box to enter the password. Trying to come up with an idea of the password Savannah would use, I glanced up at a pin board hanging above the desk on the wall.

There was a photo of Savannah and her parents. I didn't recognize the background. Right next to the image was a print-out of a highly secured building. There was a tall fence with barb wire at the top that wrapped around the facility and a guard standing at the open gate. A caption read: **Glayfield California State Prison for Men.**

I geared my attention back towards the computer. *What would Savannah use as a password? Something she cares about, something she wouldn't forget, something meaningful.* Glancing back at the billboard, I stared at the picture of her family. Her dad! Robert Bakers.

Looking back at the screen, I typed in Robert Bakers. I knew it was a long shot, but it was my only idea. It didn't work.

I needed something more meaningful to her. I knew it had to do with her dad, he was probably the most important person to her.

I typed in: D-A-D-D-Y. It worked! I was in. It may have been a silly password, but at least it wasn't too complicated. I smiled to myself. No decoding device necessary.

The screen came to life. A security video came up. Savannah hadn't closed it out before turning off her laptop the last time she was in here.

A specific video was up, waiting to be played.

I turned off the volume so no one would wake up and pushed play, and then something caught my eye.

Someone on the screen looked so familiar to me, yet I couldn't figure out who it was. He wore a mask along with a brown coat. The man spoke to Savannah. In the video Savannah moved her balance from one foot to the other. Her hands were held behind her back. The man then pulled out a weird looking gun that also looked familiar. He spoke to her from under the mask, but I couldn't hear what they were saying. I had a feeling I wouldn't like it if I did. The mask and the gun seemed so important, as if I should know exactly what they were, who it was wearing the mask. Alarms went off in my head, telling me this person was dangerous. I tried to think of who it could be, to picture something I thought I should have known.

A quick image came into my mind; a gun being pointed at me. A brick in my hand. Focusing on the image in my mind, I tried to elaborate more, but as soon as the image came into my head it was gone. A slight pain filled my head. I could feel the pressure of something hitting me, right where the bandage on my forehead used to be. Lifting my hand up to my face, I touched where the pain felt worse, remembering the scrapes and bandages I woke up with at the hospital. As quick as the pain came, it was gone. I returned to the video on the computer screen.

When the video was over, I dug through the drawers in the desk. Pencils, paper, a stapler, nothing special. The papers on the desk weren't any more interesting. Homework assignments. I got to the bottom of the pile. A yellow folder was hidden under her homework. Opening it up, I found arrest reports. Her dad's arrest reports. I squinted, trying to read something from the papers, but it was too dark. I didn't have enough time to sit under the tiny desk lamp and read. Maybe I could find the report on the T.S.O. database. I put the file back on her desk, covering it up with the other papers, and turned to face Emily.

"Let's go."

Emily nodded to me in agreement. I pushed Emily out the door and down the hall. Hopefully, with more luck, I'd have another opportunity to try again later.

We stopped in the kitchen and put the pink key back in the drawer. Returning to the living room I found Savannah fast asleep in her sleeping bag. All the girls were unaware of what Emily and I did.

Emily and I took our places in our sleeping bags. I closed my eyes with the image of the masked man in my head.

Chapter 8

Uncle Jason

For breakfast we had blueberry pancakes with whipped cream. Neither Emily nor I mentioned what happened the night before. She seemed to avoid my eye contact.

After breakfast, little by little, everyone's parents came to pick them up. I needed more time with Savannah.

Inside the bathroom, I locked the door and pulled my cell phone out. Thanks to the T.S.O. I had the best voice recording equipment available. Opening up the program, I selected the recording of my mom's voice. I would be able to use a voice changing algorithm and a cell phone number scrambler to make it look like my mom was calling someone else. Once the system was set up, I called Mrs. Bakers.

"Hello?" she said into the phone.

"Hi Julia," I said, standing in the corner of the bathroom. "I'm really sorry but my car just broke down.

My husband is at work and I can't make it over to pick up Amelia. Is there any way you could give Amelia a ride home?"

"Of course." I smiled to myself, glad the voice system was working.

"Thank you so much."

"No worries. As soon as all the other girls leave, we'll be on our way."

"Alright. No rush. I really appreciate it."

After saying a quick goodbye, I hung up the phone. It worked!

I called Mom, letting her know Mrs. Bakers was going to give me a ride. "Are you sure you don't need me to pick you up?" she asked.

"I'm sure."

"Okay, well I'll see you when you get home."

I pocketed my phone. "Let's do this," I whispered, smiling at my achievement. I felt the urge to jump, but that probably would have been a little over the top.

"Amelia?" Mrs. Bakers called out to me as I walked down the hall.

"Yes?"

"Your mom just called me. She can't make it so I'll drive you home."

"Okay." Mrs. Bakers turned away. I walked back into the living room. Now was my chance.

Everyone was gone now. I sat on the couch, waiting for Savannah to come out of her room. There was a knock at the front door. Savannah was still in her room. Mrs. Bakers was nowhere to be seen. A loud knock filled the room again. Who was here?

"Coming!" Mrs. Bakers shouted. She came into the room from the kitchen and answered the door. "Savannah, your uncle's here!" She called back, holding the door open. Mrs. Bakers' voice was anything but friendly. She stared at the person in the doorway, glaring at him. Her posture became stiff. Something was wrong.

A tall man walked into the room. His black hair was spiked, hands buried inside his long coat pockets, a serious expression on his face as he peered around the room. His gaze fell on me. I smiled at him, waving my hand in greeting. His eyebrows raised in shock at the sight of me, his right hand digging deeper into his pocket.

"Hey!" Savannah said, emerging from her room just in time. She looked at me, then at her uncle, and her brow furrowed. "Amelia, this is Uncle Jason," she said, introducing me. I stood up and made my way over. Uncle Jason never took his eyes off me. His expression changed from shock to curiosity as he raised his eyebrows, just for a moment.

"Nice to meet you." His voice was dry as sand paper. He turned away from me, not shaking my outstretched hand. "Savannah, we need to talk." I watched as he pushed her into the kitchen, away from view. Who was this guy? Was he related to Savannah's dad?

Mrs. Bakers closed the front door, shaking her head at the ground. She walked down the hallway. I watched her until she disappeared into one of the rooms. I wondered if she knew anything.

I sat on the couch for at least five minutes, staring at the photos on the walls and the brown carpet. I could have listened to their conversation, but the way Savannah's uncle looked at me left me uneasy. My stomach turned. I felt uncomfortable, sitting in the living room by myself, hushed voices coming from the kitchen.

"Savannah, it's time to go!" Mrs. Bakers called down the hall. She emerged from the hallway and now stood by the opened door, car keys in hand. I grabbed my bag and headed for the door.

A minute later Savannah came out of the kitchen, a worried look on her face. I followed Savannah out the door, wondering what had happened between her and her uncle.

"I want you gone when I get back," Mrs. Bakers shouted into the house. With that she closed and locked the front door, then took her seat at the wheel.

I didn't say anything as we pulled out of the driveway. There was an awkward silence in the air, and it had something to do with the uncle we left in the house. There was something going on with this Uncle Jason, and I was going to get to the bottom of it. Right after I stopped Savannah.

Chapter 9

The Girl With the Blond Hair

The next day at school, while sitting at the lunch tables eating a ham sandwich with the rest of my class, Savannah came up to me and sat down. She was telling everyone how much fun she had at the sleepover. It was Savannah's actual birthday, and she brought cupcakes for the choir group. Everybody was laughing about the memories of flour in my face and Savannah's cousin's way of mimicking the movie characters.

Emily quickly pulled me away from the table.

"Who was that guy on the video?" Emily asked in a hushed voice.

"I'm not sure. Now that I think of it, he kind of looked like Savannah's uncle." I thought of the man I met after the party, broad shouldered and tall. Not to mention the brown coat he wore, the same in the video. "I met him after everyone left," I explained.

41

"I can't stand school. I can't wait till summer." I was pulled out of my thoughts about Uncle Jason by the sound of my classmates' voices. I looked over at the table to find everyone smiling, some laughing, at the thought of their summers.

"Okay," Emily responded, nodding her head in thought. I couldn't help but wonder what she was thinking, why she cared so much.

"Why?" I asked, focusing on our conversation again. She seemed so curious about what happened last night. "What's going on?"

"Nothing," Emily said, smiling at me. "I just wondered if you knew anything. Come on, let's join the others." Emily grabbed my hand and pulled me back to the table, preventing me from asking any further questions.

"Summer, I can't wait!" Tony exclaimed, walking up to the group. He smiled at me, taking a seat in between me and Emily. "Good afternoon ladies," he said, looking around the table.

"We were just talking about Savannah's party," Emily explained.

"Oh, I understand, girl stuff," Tony exclaimed in a sarcastic voice. I shook my head at him. Was Tony even capable of being serious? "I guess I'll come back later then," he said. Tony winked at me as he got up from the table.

"Tony is probably one of the weirdest guys in the class," one of the girls said. "He never makes any sense."

"I agree," Emily said, nudging me in the shoulder.

I thought of Tony's pranks, wondering just how irritated he made Emily. Why did I remember who he was and not her? I let the thoughts of my case leave my head for

42

a moment. If only I could remember what it was like to not have a secret identity, to not know about the T.S.O. Once school was over, I would be able to focus on my case a lot more.

After school that day, I went back to my office at T.S.O. headquarters. I wanted to see if I could find Mr. Bakers' arrest in the records. I logged into the database on my computer, putting in my access code. I went to the main search engine. Robert Bakers.

Apparently, Bakers was a common name, but after a few minutes of searching I found who I was looking for.

A mug shot of Savannah's dad filled the screen. His hair was as black as Savannah's, in a tousled mess atop his head. His eyes looked sad and tired, not guilty. Just brown, sad eyes staring into the camera. I could tell by his features, the bags under his eyes, that he was tired when they took the photo. His lips curled into a lonely frown.

I scrolled down, finding a digital copy of his arrest report. His last known residence recorded was the same as Savannah's, the same place I was only days ago. The reporting officer was Mrs. Steinfeld. Emily's mom. The report explained, he was arrested for the embezzlement and theft of government weapons along with their mechanical system layouts. The report didn't clarify what type of weapon he stole.

Putting my hands over my face, I thought for a moment. What type of weapon? Why wasn't that information included? This was a top-secret database, there would be no reason to exclude the information. Not just anybody had access to the database. I slouched back in my chair, looking up at my computer screen for answers that weren't there. How was this information going to help me stop Savannah?

A shadow flew past my office door. I sat up in my chair, fully alert now. Someone was looking into my office, then ran off when they realized I was there.

"Hey! Come back here!" I shouted as I jumped up towards the door, turning abruptly around the corner. My calls went unanswered. The mysterious person broke into a run as I followed behind her.

I ran down the hallway trying to catch up to her, all thoughts of Mr. Bakers leaving my mind. Her hair was light blond and swayed from side to side in beat with her footsteps. Well, that narrows it down, I thought. It could be anyone, anyone with access to the headquarters.

I continued chasing her down the hall and tried to get a better look at her. Her clothes were as mundane as possible. A pair of blue jeans and a black T-shirt. I couldn't get a good look at her shoes as she lifted her feet, only showing me the black soles on the bottom.

At the end of the hall she turned left, then right. People peeked out of their offices and the rooms we passed as they wondered what all the commotion was about. No one seemed uneasy at the sight of the girl I was chasing.

"Come back!" I shouted again. The girl kept running. She led me down a small flight of stairs, never looking back at me. I kept running. She pushed a trashcan down trying to block my path. I jumped over it just in time to see her knock down another.

As I made my way through the maze of trashcans, a cart full of papers and files rolled out of an office door directly into my path. The young man guiding it had no chance to avoid me and I couldn't slowdown in time to dodge his cart.

Boom! I crashed right into the cart and went tumbling head over heels in a cloud of paper and envelopes onto the floor. "Hey!" the boy shouted lying on the floor covered in loose files of paper.

"Sorry!" I shouted, as I jumped up and ran down the hall.

Just as I found the mysterious girl again, she went through a door that led to the private subway. As I ran to the door, it slammed in my face. "Come on!" I shouted into the air. When the door opened, she was nowhere to be seen. I entered the platform just in time to see the subway train accelerating down the track, its sounds slowly fading.

I missed her. The girl with blond hair. She had to be spying on me. The real question was why.

Chapter 10

Meeting with the Police

School had ended for the day and with my backpack over my shoulder I headed towards the main entrance. Not a lot of students were in the halls anymore. As I passed the computer lab, I noticed the lights were on. They weren't supposed to be. Peering through the small window on the door, I saw Savannah. She was seated in the farthest row from the door in front of a lit computer screen. I needed to talk to her. I opened the door, walking towards Savannah.

"What's up?" I asked as I walked down the rows of computers.

Savannah quickly turned off the computer monitor. All I caught was a glimpse of blue prints, at least, that's what it looked like.

"Nothing, just finishing homework, you know," she said sounding a little nervous.

"Cool, but the classroom is supposed to be closed. How did you get inside?" I made sure my voice was full of excitement. "The door is supposed to be locked." I did my best to sound casual without making her upset. If she didn't trust me, she wouldn't reveal anything.

"I know." Savannah's hands couldn't lay still. She kept refolding her hands in her lap. "The door was unlocked and when the computer teacher came by, he gave me a few more minutes."

"What are you working on?"

"Um." She took longer to come up with something than she should have. Whatever she said would be a lie. One of the first things we learn at the T.S.O. was to come up with things on the fly. We could never be caught. "Science. My teacher is having me do a project on something. I was creating a presentation," she said, continuing to fidget in her seat.

"That's cool. Can I see?" I asked, putting on a smile.

"Um, it's really not finished yet. I practically just started."

"Oh, well that's alright. Maybe next time."

"Yeah, maybe." She gave a slight smile, waiting for me to leave.

"Well, I will see you tomorrow then. Good luck on your project." I turned and began to walk away, hesitant on leaving.

After closing the door, I peered through the window once more. Savannah turned on the monitor and continued working. She took a deep breath. I really didn't want to make her upset. This case should have been easy, but it was proving to be harder than usual. Why couldn't I bring myself to pry any information out of her? Was I losing my touch? I thought about my memory loss. Did that have anything to do with my lack of persistence?

I left school, wondering what else I could do to get this case solved. Once the bus driver dropped me off at the house, I put my backpack inside and decided what I was going to do. I had two hours before my parents would be home, time I usually spent doing this kind of thing anyways.

I walked down the sidewalk, not wanting to draw attention to myself as I headed for the police station where Emily's mom worked. I had to talk to her. I just didn't know how I was supposed to start the conversation.

After jogging the twenty-minute walk to the station, no longer affected by my knee injury, I entered the building through a revolving door. The jogging felt good, refreshing. I walked through the lobby and took the elevator to the third floor. I was about to open Mrs. Steinfeld's office door when I heard voices inside.

"Mom, I can't tell her. Ms. Blanchard says so. I want to, I think it would help, but she won't let me," Emily explained to her mom.

I wondered what they were talking about, but didn't want to wait any longer to get my questions answered. I knocked on the door.

Upon seeing my face, Emily gave her mom a nervous glance.

"Hi," I said in a calm voice.

"Hello Amelia," Mrs. Steinfeld responded. "How are you?"

"I'm fine. I have to talk to you though."

"What can I do for you?" Mrs. Steinfeld said to me

in a sweet sort of way. My parents were friends with Mrs. Steinfeld before Emily and I were born. She was like my second mom sometimes. At least, I think so. That's what it feels like, considering I can't really remember.

"It's about something a little personal and I can't exactly tell my parents."

"Aww," she said as she motioned Emily out of the room. "What's wrong?" It wasn't unusual for me to come to her with something personal, not that I did very often.

"Well, I need to talk to you about some cases you wrote reports on and the security breach on your computer. Please don't ask why, it's really important."

"I'm sorry Amelia, but that information is confidential," Mrs. Steinfeld glanced at the door. I think I caught her off guard. I could understand why though, coming to her about her job wasn't something I usually did either, not that I could recall.

"Please," I pleaded.

"Well, the last major case I worked on was on Mr. Bakers. I believe that's Savannah's dad, right?"

"Do you know why someone would have wanted to steal the information he did?" I asked, unable to stand still.

"How do you know about the information he stole?" she asked. Her voice was calm, but something was off.

"That's not important," I replied, trying to sound convincing. Maybe I shouldn't have led with classified knowledge about his arrest.

"I believe it is important if you want any information from me," Mrs. Steinfeld replied, remaining calm the entire time.

I stood up straighter and steadied my breathing. My heart was pounding in a way I couldn't slow down. "Okay, I'm sorry. I'm doing a school report and I was wondering if you had any information I could use," I lied.

"Well, in my report, I had lots of information on what he stole from the government and everything, but you know I can't share those details with you. It's extremely classified. I'm sorry Amelia."

"That's alright; I guess that in a way I was kind of expecting that. Thanks though." What was I thinking coming here? All that information was in the arrest files. I already read all of that. Something inside me told me it was missing information. My answers wouldn't come from Mrs. Steinfeld.

"No problem. Was there anything else you had questions about?"

"No, that was all." I smiled at her, doing my best to not spark too many questions in her.

"Well, I'll see you later then Amelia. Oh, tell Emily she can come back in, will you? Thanks," she said with a smile.

I left the office making sure I told Emily she could go back inside. I didn't know what I was supposed to do at all. Nothing made sense to me. My thoughts were like a tangled necklace. I didn't know where it started, ended, or how to unravel it.

Chapter 11

Staying at the Steinfeld's

School would be out next week. Tomorrow was Sunday and I'd finally be able to sleep in, at least I thought I could sleep in.

"Come on honey, get dressed we're going to be late!" Mom said, walking into my room.

"Late for what?" I asked, covering my eyes as Mom opened the curtains.

"You're staying over at Emily's for the week, or possibly longer. I'm not totally sure what your father has planned." Her words came out rushed. Mom was stressing herself out.

"What do you mean?"

"Amelia, I told you yesterday, and last week. Your father and I are going to Oregon for his business trip. We're not sure how long we're going to be there and Mrs. Steinfeld offered to have you stay at her house for as long as we need. Now, get packing. We leave in an hour for the airport so you better be ready."

She left my room, shutting the door with a loud bang behind her, leaving me stunned. I never heard her talk so fast. There has been so much going on it must have slipped my mind.

The more I thought about it, the more I figured this could be a good thing. No parents there to keep me from leaving the house. Now I just have to get past Mrs. Steinfeld and Emily. I thought of Emily's dad, but I couldn't think of what he looked like. He was in the navy and lived on a base out of the country. It had been a long time since I saw him last. He wouldn't be at the house.

I threw the covers off and jumped out of bed, grabbing my suitcase from the closet.

"Bye honey, have a nice time!" Mom said as she drove away after dropping me off at Emily's.

"Bye Mom, bye Dad, have fun. See you soon!" I shouted as they drove around the corner out of sight.

I walked inside with Emily and put my stuff down on her bed. "This is going to be so much fun!" Emily started, "I can't believe your parents are letting you stay with us for over a week. What do you want to do first Amelia, watch a movie, play outside, or do makeovers?"

"Actually," I said cutting her off, "there are some things I have to do this week."

"That's okay, I'll come with you. My mom won't mind us being out. She spends a lot of her time at home working in the basement. Where do you need to go?"

"I don't have to leave now." Emily's shoulders slumped. Did she know I was hiding something? "How about we watch a movie first?" I offered. I didn't have access to a computer here and my laptop at the T.S.O. would give me access to just about any information I wanted. How was I going to get rid of Emily? It sounded rude, ditching my best friend, but I didn't have much of a choice. "I'm all yours except for one errand that I have to run on my own. But I can go anytime."

"Oh, okay. Well, why don't you go and just do whatever you need to do and I'll just tell my mom you haven't arrived yet. We can watch a movie when you get back. Where do you need to go anyway? Are you sure I can't come?" she asked with pleading eyes.

"Not this time," I said, letting out a laugh at her bombardment of questions.

"Fiinnne," she complained, dragging out the word to show her disappointment.

I made my way down the street, casually glancing behind me to make sure Emily wasn't following. Breaking into a run, I turned another corner and crossed the street to the park. It took me longer to get there than usual. I would have to put in some more physical training at the headquarters. Why did injuries have to mess with my strength as well as my head?

At the park bathrooms I walked around the facility to the maintenance room. I plugged in the four-digit code and walked inside. There were pipes along the walls and stored supplies for those who took care of the park and restrooms.

Walking over to the only empty corner in the storage room, I put my hand up to the wall. A small scanner appeared and scanned my hand. Just like the elevator in the alley by the parking structure, a square platform began lowering into the ground, and a new one slid into its place. The elevator lowered me about forty feet down. I made my way down a dimly lit hallway that let out onto the T.S.O. subway station platform. Boarding the train, I took a seat by the window. Not very many people were on the train.

After riding a short distance, the train came to a stop at a small platform. I walked through a door that lead to the T.S.O. headquarters and made my way to my office.

I decided to see if I could find any more information on Savannah and her dad inside the T.S.O.'s computer database. The T.S.O. database contained information on practically anyone and anything you can think of and more. What type of connections would Mr. Bakers have had?

Sitting at my desk I opened up the database. Before I could even put my access code in someone sped past my office door. I heard the sound of footsteps quickly fading away. This time I tip-toed out my office and secretly followed behind the girl.

Her hair was pure blond like last time. The mystery girl was wearing pink and black sneakers with a pink shirt with dark blue jeans. Now that I thought of it, Emily was wearing a pink shirt today. "It can't be her," I told myself, "otherwise Emily would tell me."

She must have noticed me following her because she picked up speed. I sped up my pace so I wouldn't fall too far behind. She took the same route through the office as she did the last time. I followed her all the way to the subway station. Bursting through the door, I ran out onto the platform. The entrance to the train closed. The girl ducked down inside the train, probably lying on the floor so I couldn't see her. The doors wouldn't open again. I watched the train pass by, it's wheels running on the track laughing at my failure of catching up as it departed from the station.

I headed back into the office, figuring I should just head back to Emily's. I couldn't believe I lost the mystery-girl twice.

As I arrived, Mrs. Steinfeld came upstairs from the basement with Emily walking right behind her. I grabbed a water bottle from the fridge, noticing Emily's pink t-shirt and blond hair. Was it her I was chasing at headquarters? But she wasn't a T.S.O. Agent. Was she?

Chapter 12

Breaking and Entering

Sunday, Mrs. Steinfeld made pancakes and eggs for breakfast.

"So, you going anywhere else today?" Emily asked, excitement dripping in her tone. "Can I tag along?" She took another bite of her pancakes, stuffing them in her mouth.

"No. I'll be here all day." I took a bite, avoiding eye contact.

"Come on! We've known each other since what, forever? If anyone knows you the best, it's me. What do you have planned?" She smiled at me, like a puppy begging for a treat. I tried to think of how long I've known her, when we met, but nothing came to mind. Part of me felt angry for not knowing Emily as well as she knew me. The other part just felt lost.

"Fine," I said smiling at her. "I told you before, I'm

all yours."

After a morning full of mundane activities, Emily and I grabbed our bikes and headed for the streets. I wanted to see if Savannah was home. We needed to get inside that room again. I needed to re-watch that video. Breaking and entering may be illegal, but as a secret agent we must go to extreme measures to accomplish what needed to be done.

"Why are you carrying a bag with you?" I asked. "You don't even know where we're going."

"I just brought some supplies. I want to be ready for anything, even if I don't know what it is yet. Thanks for letting me come."

"No problem, but you can't tell anyone where we're going or what we're doing. You got that?"

"Yes Ma'am!" Emily said, taking one hand off her bike's steering wheel and pretending to salute me.

We continued pedaling in silence.

"Isn't this Savannah's neighborhood?" Emily said as we rode onto her street.

"Yes, it is." I continued pedaling, Emily right beside me. I locked up the anxious feelings. This is going to work. I'm going to get the information I need.

"What are we doing here? Isn't she out of town this weekend?" Emily asked as we pulled into Savannah's driveway.

"I know, but it's really important," I stated. Climbing off my bike I looked over at Emily.

"Just don't get me in trouble. My mom would get upset if she found out what we were up to," Emily said, a little nervous at the situation. I felt bad for bringing Emily along, for having to do this in the first place, but I didn't feel like I had any other choice. I usually enjoyed the thrilling field work that came with my job, but I was more nervous than excited this time.

We hid our bikes behind some bushes in the front yard and made our way to the front door. I knocked, hoping no one was home.

To my luck, no one answered. Just to be sure though, I peeked through the window next to the front door. No one was inside.

One side of Savannah's house had a fence around it, the other was open. I guided Emily alongside the open part of the house. A row of bushes covered the first few feet on the side of the house. I stood between the leaves as I peered through the windows. No one was inside. I even checked for security cameras. If they had cameras outside, they hid them pretty well.

Going back to the front of the house, I tried the door. Locked.

Sticking my hand into my pocket I pulled out what appeared to be a credit card. It was a special card for just such an occasion, a gift from the T.S.O. I pushed a tiny button on the card within one of the numbers and held it flat against the door lock. After scanning the lock, the front half of the card folded itself into the shape of a key.

With a small squeaking sound, I turned the key inside the lock and the door opened. Emily wasn't even paying attention to what I was doing. Her eyes gazed upon the empty street.

"This is totally illegal," I heard Emily whispering under her breath as she looked up and down the street. "Finally, we're getting somewhere!" I couldn't help but laugh a little, wondering why she was so excited to be doing this. "What are we doing exactly?" she asked, turning to face me as I opened the door.

"It's hard to explain. I have to look at something. Something important. We're a team, right? You've got to trust me." I looked right at her, hoping she understood how serious I was.

"I trust you."

"Good."

I turned and walked straight for the kitchen, careful not to make a sound. I found the pink key we used to open up the door to Savannah's back room in the same drawer I did the night of the sleepover.

Emily and I headed down the hall. My key card only worked once every hour, and it needed to recharge.

We entered the room and Emily turned off the laser system. I headed straight for the computer.

"How did Savannah even know where to buy a laser beam system?" Emily asked as the computer loaded.

"I think she made this one. Savannah's good with that sort of stuff." I sat down at the chair in front of the desk.

"Why are we doing this? This reminds me of when we came in here during the sleepover."

I didn't answer her, just entered the password on the computer. After finding the video we saw earlier, I found a video of Emily and I walking down the hall, in and out of the kitchen, and opening the door to the room we were in now. I deleted the video, frustrated with myself for not noticing the cameras inside the house.

Looking up to the pin board on the wall above the

desk I saw a picture of a stone that wasn't there last time we were here. The stone was red, probably smooth to the touch, and had a glowing reflection around it. It had an image inside it, like four lines crossing each other to make an intricate diamond shape, although the stone itself was a misshapen oval.

There was another picture of a diamond necklace that looked familiar to me.

At the corner of the pinboard there were several photos of what appeared to be a maximum-security prison. The same prison probably as the other photo of the tall fence, which was still there.

"Come on, let's watch the video before anyone comes home, assuming that's why we're in here," Emily said.

Just as Emily finished speaking, we heard the front door unlock. "Dang it!" I whispered.

"Don't worry, I have a plan." Emily took off her backpack and opened up the front pocket. She pulled out a striped pink and blue flash drive. Emily plugged it into the computer and began downloading the security video.

"Why did you bring a flash drive?" I asked under my breath.

"I wanted to be ready for anything. And you better be glad I brought it." She dragged her finger on the touch pad, uploading the video.

"We should probably hide," I said, listening to the footsteps get louder.

We ducked behind the same filing cabinet I hid behind the last time. At the last possible second, I turned back and shut the laptop's lid as the flash drive continued downloading from the computer. Emily slid a paper over the top of the flash drive.

I could hear footsteps in the hall getting louder and louder. My blood pounded in my head with every thumping footstep.

The door opened.

"Savannah." It was a man's voice. "She never remembers to lock the door. If anyone ever steals this equipment, I'll kill her." The man turned off the lights and activated the laser system. I wanted to turn around and see who it was, but he would have seen us. He closed the door and walked away. His voice was familiar, I couldn't match it to a face.

"That was a close one." I whispered.

With one of the beams only a foot from the space Emily and I occupied, I rolled onto my back. I moved through the lasers, bending, turning and flipping as I worked my way to the front of the room. Back at the T.S.O. training camp we had simulations just like this for this very purpose. I slid up against the wall, feeling with my hand for the off switch.

"That was awesome!" Emily said. "Where did you learn how to do that?"

"Oh, at um, at gymnastics." I turned around, able to move freely with the system shut down.

"You never took gymnastics."

"My mom taught me. She got this DVD that taught me some weird gymnastics and stuff." I don't think I've ever said anything cheesier. It was a sad excuse, but it ended the conversation. Maybe I really was losing my touch.

I hurried to the desk and pulled out the flash drive,

putting it in my pants pocket. I temporarily shut down the surveillance cameras, programing them to come back on in ten minutes. I snatched a photo of the pin board above the desk and headed to the door. Emily turned on the laser system. I snapped a picture of the room before walking out.

We stopped in the kitchen and put the pink key back in the drawer. Continuing down the hallway, I saw a man in the nearest room. His back was turned so his face stayed hidden. Emily and I sneaked our way past the door as quietly as we could.

We were almost to the front door when we heard footsteps coming from the hallway. The man was coming in our direction. I grabbed Emily's hand and pulled her into the nearest room. It was Savannah's bedroom. Emily and I ran to the window as silent as mice. Sliding the window open, I took out the screen and we climbed out.

Just as I finished putting the screen back in place the man peered into Savannah's room. Emily grabbed my arm and pulled me to the ground and out of sight. We were crouched in the dirt behind bushes as we scooted our way towards the front yard.

We retrieved our bikes from the bushes and made a hasty retreat down the street.

"That was awesome! I can't believe we did that. Why exactly did we do that? Why can't you tell me what's really going on? Seriously. It's getting old Amelia," Emily exclaimed.

"It's complicated. Someday though, it'll make perfect sense. I promise."

"Okay. I just hope that time is soon."

"Hey, how about we ride to the park? We can hang out there. The ice cream parlor is there too," I offered.

"Sounds fun, but you're paying."

"Deal," I laughed. "We can look at that flash drive when we get back." I didn't want Emily getting caught up in this. Yes, she could be a big help, but it was too dangerous. I couldn't put that on her, not to mention I couldn't even remember her from before my accident.

As we rode down the street, I thought about telling Emily my secret. How would she take it? What's the worst that could happen?

As we continued riding my head started throbbing. I could hear my heartbeat as everything slowed down. The rode in front of me became blurry.

The entire world began spinning. I could hear Emily's voice over and over again, "Amelia, Amelia! Wake up. .."

I blacked out.

Everything was blurry. I took a moment to refocus my thoughts, to calm down. I still felt uneasy. As my vision cleared and my head stopped aching, I could tell I was in a theme park. My parents and I were walking around, heading towards a rollercoaster. I held a bag of blue cotton candy, Dad constantly taking more out of the bag.

At a bench nearby I saw someone peeking through holes somebody cut out of his newspaper, and two guys that were leading a nearby game were all staring in my direction. They looked angry to me, and the guy with the newspaper seemed to be taking pictures between sentences and crossword puzzles.

The phone in my pocket started vibrating. Telling my parents I had to go to the restroom, I walked around the corner near a hot dog stand into a small, dirty alley. Nervous butterflies filled my stomach and my chest rose and fell with anxious breaths.

I pulled a cell phone out of my pocket, just as it was ready to stop ringing. Pulling it up to my ear, I answered the call. "What's up?"

Chapter 13
Agent Powell

"Amelia? Can you hear me?" Emily said as I slowly opened my eyes.

"Where are we? What happened?" I grabbed my head and pulled myself up into a sitting position. The image inside the alley, inside the park, was completely gone. It must have been a memory.

I was too tired to completely worry about it.

"You're fine Amelia." I heard a voice say. All I could see was a bright glare as someone pointed a light into my eyes.

"Amelia?... *Agent Z?* My name is Dr. Powell. Your friend here called 911 and said you fainted. You can trust me. You're in good hands," he whispered in a very calm voice. As my vision cleared, I could see a gentle smile on his face, the scruffiness of a beard beginning to show.

"What did you call me?" All I could think of was what I saw. It had to be a dream, but it felt so much like it actually happened.

"Please, don't speak. You might have hurt your head and I don't want it to get any worse than it already is. You've suffered enough head trauma this year."

I rubbed my fingers over my new scars, but I still couldn't recall what had really happened. Emily and her mom were in a hospital room with me, but they weren't the only people there.

Ms. Blanchard was standing in the back of the room with Tony. With all tiredness aside, I was ready to jump out of the bed.

I had a major headache. What was going on? Why did I faint? "Can I just rest for a moment?" I asked.

"Alright, but I need to speak with you first," Dr. Powell responded. After everyone left the room, I sat up and Dr. Powell sat in a chair next to the bed. "Agent Z," Dr. Powell started.

"Why are you calling me agent?" I asked, wondering just how much he really knew. Did I talk in my sleep or something? I sure hope the answer to that was "or something."

"Come on Amelia. You are an agent of the T.S.O. I'm also known as Agent Powell," he said.

Taking off his glasses, his eyes changed color from a dark hazel to a brown. I knew the gadget he was using belonged to the organization, but I didn't know Agent Powell. "I work in the infirmary. It's okay if you don't remember," the doctor said genuinely. I was getting used to not remembering things, but it still bothered me.

"Well then, why exactly did I faint?"

"There is something you need to know Amelia." He became very serious. The smile left his face as he lowered his eyebrows. "Ever since your accident you've experienced memory loss."

"I know," I said, rolling my eyes. "I've kind of figured that out." I sat up in the hospital bed.

"When you first ended up in the hospital it was because of an attack. You were trying to track down someone known as Dr. Doom."

I laughed a little when he said this. Who would pick that as a criminal name?

"He's the one who knocked you out in the first place. He had some sort of weapon. Don't worry, he has been apprehended. He's being held in Glayfield Prison."

"The Glayfield Prison?" I thought of the picture on the pin board in Savannah's office.

"Yes, Glayfield Prison. That's not important though," Agent Powell insisted. I wanted to think otherwise. "You need to trust Emily."

"Trust her with what?"

"You know what I'm talking about. It's alright if she finds out. Just trust her and when the time comes, you'll understand why."

"Okay, why can't you tell me?"

"Ms. Blanchard's orders, but that's not important either. You need to focus on your assignment. If you ever start feeling really tired, and get a major headache, just slow down and focus. It might be a memory coming back. Ms. Blanchard won't like that I told you about your amnesia.

You know she can be a little strict."

Agent Powell put his glasses back on and let the others back in the room.

Why was Ms. Blanchard being so strict? She had to have a reason for her orders. I just wish I knew what it was.

Tony began talking about his summer plans, a camping trip he couldn't wait for out in the desert. I didn't pay attention to his story, but he didn't seem to notice. As he spoke, I watched Emily, who wasn't paying much attention to him either. She looked concerned and kept quiet in her seat.

"It's going to be great!" Tony exclaimed. "I can't wait!"

"That's great Tony," I said dryly, wishing I was more enthusiastic for him.

Once we got back to the Steinfeld's there was a phone call from my parents.

"Amelia, are you alright?" Dad asked. I could hear the concern in his unsteady voice.

"I'm fine," I said as I nodded my head in agreement. But he couldn't see me through the phone.

"Do we need to come home?" he asked. I imagined the wrinkles on his forehead as he spoke, as he pressed his fingers to his temples.

"Dad, please, I'm alright. I'm fine, really."

"I'm just glad you're okay."

"Me too," I responded, letting a smile cross my face.

"Are you sure you don't want us to come home?"

"I'm sure," I said. "Finish your trip."

After sharing with him about school and listening to him share about all his board meetings, I hung up the phone.

Emily and I plugged the flash drive into her laptop once we were settled in her room. The downloaded video from Savannah's computer appeared on the screen.

"Push play," I told Emily, leaning over her shoulder to see the computer. Her hands shook over the keys for a second before she hit the button.

As the video started playing, I listened to their conversation.

Savannah stood in the hallway of her house with whom I believe was her uncle, Jason. It was a different video from last time. As the video played, their simple conversation turned into an argument.

"Savannah, you can't back out now!" he shouted at her. "I need your skills. I wouldn't have been able to take down that agent without that weapon." The man paused for a moment, taking in a breath. "None of this would have happened if it wasn't for you."

"I regret doing that," Savannah said. Even through the camera feed I could tell she was holding back tears.

"She knew too much! It had to be done. Just be glad she isn't dead." Shivers went through my spine at the rough sound of the man's voice.

The sound began screeching as the feed on the camera started to glitch.

"What happened?" I asked, as only the image continued to play on the computer.

"I don't know," Emily responded. "Maybe it didn't

download properly. We did leave in a hurry."

I watched the video as Savannah's uncle pulled a ski mask over his head that sent shivers down my spine. It seemed all too familiar now. It had to be the same one the man in the video was wearing the first time we saw it. If only I could remember where else I've seen it before. What agent was he talking about? I was missing a piece of the puzzle.

"I don't understand," I said to Emily.

"I think we're missing something," Emily pondered. I could hear the curiosity in her voice. "I mean, who knows what he's talking about."

Chapter 14

Monday, March 21st

Three Days Before Amelia's Accident

I was riding home on my bike from the T.S.O. I turned the corner, entering my neighborhood. I glanced at the same old statue across the street that I have passed a thousand times before on my way home.

I waved to an elderly woman watering her plants near the sidewalk. She had gray, silvery hair put up into a bun and calm, gentle hazel eyes that peered through large glasses. The elderly woman, like myself, worked for the T.S.O. She helped watch the front desk at the entrance I usually used to get into headquarters.

Passing the woman's house, I heard a dog bark, then another. I turned right onto First Avenue and saw something flash in the corner of my eye. I didn't pay much attention to it. I just wanted to get home. I was angry at myself, angry for not knowing how to finish my assignment.

A moment later something hit the back tire of my bike, causing me to lose control. The front handle bar spun around and I flew off the bike head over heels before I could do anything. I rolled to the ground with the bike landing on top of me.

With a groan I pushed the bike off and started to pull myself up off the ground. I looked back in the direction I had come from.

Just a few feet away, a familiar figure was approaching. He wore a ski mask that I recognized all too well.

"What do you want *'Dr. Doom'*? You know, I still think you have the most unintelligent name for a petty thief. It's such a cartoon name," I teased, trying to upset Doom, who was much more than a simple 'petty thief'. My heart skipped a beat, excited by the encounter. I had been trying to track him down for days now. I had started to think he fled the state.

"The necklace, and your life," he responded. "I'm tired of you getting in the way of my plans. It's time I do something about that." Dr. Doom had stolen an invaluable necklace made of gold and diamonds. It was worth a lot of money. I'd retrieved the stolen jewelry and returned it to the museum it rightfully belonged to only two weeks ago.

"The necklace is gone Doom… and you'll never get it back." I smiled, opening my arms out to my side, egging him on as I took a step backwards.

Dr. Doom pulled out an odd-looking gun from inside his huge coat pocket. The time for words was over. I lunged at him, grabbing his wrist and twisting so the odd-looking weapon dropped out of his hand. Once it hit the ground I kicked it away, still holding onto his arm. The weapon slid down the street.

Dr. Doom turned abruptly, causing me to lose my grip, and tried to get to his misshapen gun. Before he could move, I grabbed his left arm, flipping him in the air and making him land flat on his back. He groaned in pain at the impact. As I turned around, attempting to retrieve his weapon, Doom grabbed my feet, causing me to fall down to the ground next to him.

Rolling over to face him, I ignored the pain in my leg, punched Doom square in the nose and quickly sprung back to my feet. I found a loose brick from a planter next to us on the sidewalk. I aimed the brick at Dr. Doom just as he grabbed hold of his gun. He aimed the weapon at me and pulled the trigger.

I saw a quick flash of a bright white and blue light. I fell to the ground with a throbbing pain in my leg, even worse than it had been a few moments before. He fired again. I dropped the brick, unable to hold onto it. It hit me in the head before landing with a thud on the ground. The faint sound of sirens in the distance filled my ears as I lost consciousness.

Chapter 15

Alexis

I wondered if my parents would still cut their trip short due to my second time of being in the hospital even though I assured them I was alright. I had got to get this case moving.

"Dr. - Agent Powell," I began as I walked into the main office area of the T.S.O., glad I was able to get away from Emily for a while. She had to run some errands with her mom and they were okay with me resting at the house. At least that's what they thought I was doing. "Agent Powell, I need a favor."

"Yes, Agent Z? What is it? And how are you feeling?" He looked up at me from his desk with his usual gentle smile, still holding a pen in his hand.

"I'm fine. I need to get some information about the case I'm working on, but the lady that has the information is my best friend's mom and she won't give it to me, even if I do show her some sort of ID, I doubt she will reveal anything."

"Amelia, I understand, but don't you think that's a little unnecessary? The answer will come in time," Agent Powell said.

"But I don't have any more time," I exclaimed, dragging my hands across my face. "I need answers now and I feel like I'm running out of options."

"Amelia," Agent Powell started, "You need to stop worrying so much."

"I'm not worried," I said, realizing how worried I actually was when I said it. Ms. Blanchard has been acting weird. Something was off with Emily, but I couldn't bring myself to say anything, especially since I couldn't remember her from before my accident. The case was going nowhere and my head was spinning in a thousand different directions. After a moment of thinking about everything I've had to deal with, I took a deep breath. "Okay, maybe I am a little overwhelmed."

"It's alright to not know what's going to happen," Agent Powell reassured me. "You just have to have faith in yourself and in your friends.

"Thanks, Agent Powell," I said, realizing how worked up I actually was. He was right. I needed to calm down.

I left the infirmary and headed to my small office, still unsure what I was going to do. Opening up the T.S.O. database I typed in Mrs. Steinfeld, wondering if the database had any information about her cases.

This is what I found:

"Chief of Police for Glayfield California, Mrs.

Angela Steinfeld has recently solved twenty-three highly classified cases in the past four years of being on the job."

Scrolling down the page with all the known information about Mrs. Steinfeld's cases I found a list of some of her most famous reports pertaining to the T.S.O. Looking at the different folders a little more, I found what I was looking for. A folder titled *Mr. Bakers.*

"What? It's empty?" I complained. The folder had nothing in it. No information, no pictures. The only information I found was this.

My apologies to those looking for this information. This case has not yet been added to the page. No information can be given out on this particular topic until later notice...

That must be because Mrs. Steinfeld was hacked. The agency took down classified information for security reasons.

"Well, that's upsetting." I leaned back in my chair and the wheels rolled back a few inches.

"What's upsetting?" A voice said from the door to my office.

I looked up to a face I haven't seen in a long time. "Alexis?" Standing there at the door was one of my old friends that I graduated with at the T.S.O. training camp two years ago. I haven't seen her in years, and there she was, standing right in front of me, now, of all possible times.

Alexis, or Agent Mills, had light brown hair and

hazel eyes. She was wearing black boots with black leggings and a leather jacket along with fingerless gloves, her usual attire. Her black field uniform looked perfect on her olive skin.

"What's up with you lately?" She said to me as she came in and took a seat on the other side of my desk. "I heard you were in an accident, maybe even some memory loss."

"That's what they tell me. Just working on another case."

"An invisible battle scar, well, we can't all be that lucky," Alexis said. Back at camp she fell from a twenty-foot rock wall during training. She now has a scar from the required stitches on the inside of her left calf. And the camp installed safety mats on the training course.

"I don't know," I responded. "It seems to be causing problems with my current case." I smiled at her. I didn't want Alexis to see how much I was conflicted with my current situation. She was always so tough. She never let her emotions show. I felt like I had to be the same way right now. "Nothing I can't handle."

"Now there's the Amelia I remember." I gave a little laugh.

"How have you been?" I asked. "I thought you were stationed in Ohio."

"I'm here on business. Ms. Blanchard said you might have some information for me, about a red diamond. Very important."

"I don't know anything about a red diamond. But I did see a picture of one when I was -" I stopped, not knowing if I could tell Alexis what Emily and I discovered at Savannah's place. An image of the stone pinned to the

77

wall in Savannah's office came into my head, vivid and clear. It hadn't seemed important at the time. After all, it was just a rock. Wasn't it?

"I saw a picture of one at a friend's house," I continued, "But how did Ms. Blanchard know that? I haven't given any reports yet."

"I don't know, but please let me know if you find out anything else on the rock. In the wrong hands it can be quite dangerous. We'll have to catch up later, before I leave."

"Will do," I said to her.

"Talk to you later. I've got to get going," Alexis said as she disappeared from the doorway.

Chapter 16

I'm a Secret Agent

Back at school, I ran into Savannah during my lunch break. "Hey Savannah. Um, can I talk to you?"

"Sure."

I wrung my hands together. I couldn't wait anymore. "I need to talk to you about your uncle."

Savannah took a deep breath and she shook her head, as if to ignore my question.

"Savannah you need to talk to me. What are you up to?"

Savannah's eyes started to water and she looked down at the ground, still shaking her head. I noticed her tugging her shirt sleeve over closer to her hand. "Not here. After school, we'll talk," she said, her voice wavering, folding and unfolding her hands repetitively. "Meet me at the bus stop." Savannah turned and left without another word.

I nodded at her even though she didn't see. My heart started racing. Finally, I was going to get some answers.

As school was ending, I saw Savannah walk towards the parking lot. How am I supposed to do this without Emily? After all, she's helped me get this far. I thought about what Dr. Powell said back at headquarters.

You know what? No more secrets.

I ran towards the lunch tables knowing she would be hanging out in her regular spot, waiting for me so we could board the bus together. I found her sitting reading a book and eating apple slices. Emily lifted her head, catching sight of me as I ran over. She closed the book and grabbed her backpack from beside her.

"Hey, Emily I need you to come with me."

"Are we going somewhere besides back to the house?" Emily asked.

"I'm going to talk to Savannah. You know how we kind of broke into her house?" I felt nervous as I asked the question, butterflies in my stomach.

"I remember." She gave me a suspicious look.

"She wants to talk to me and I need you there too."

"What exactly is going on? Come on Amelia, no more secrets."

"That's why I'm here Emily. I'm here to explain."

"Well then by all means," she flung her hand out in exasperation, "go ahead, explain."

"Okay," I started with a deep breath, but Emily didn't let me finish.

"It was totally bazaar breaking into her house!" Emily said.

"Well you seemed to enjoy it," I smirked.

"Maybe a little. So, spill." She crossed her arms and smiled.

"I'm a secret agent." I said it bluntly and as quickly as I could.

"Like, an undercover spy or something?" Her eyes grew wide.

"Yeah, something like that."

"For the T.S.O., right?"

"Right. Wait, what!?" How on earth did Emily know about the T.S.O.? Emily started laughing.

"Wow, your memory is everywhere isn't it?" She smiled at me. I stared at her, not answering, eyes wide. What was happening? "Come on Amelia. We used to be partners."

The moment she said the word partners something clicked in my head.

I remembered. I remembered Emily and I heading home from training sessions at the T.S.O., back when we first started. Not everything made sense, but I knew she was telling the truth.

"Why didn't you tell me? This would have been so much easier!" I said.

"Ms. Blanchard's orders. She thought if you just focused on your assignment things would be easier. You would have fewer things to worry about."

"What is her problem?" I asked, still taking in the

81

facts that Emily revealed.

"I'm not sure." Emily stuffed another apple slice into her mouth.

"Well, we need to go. Savannah is waiting for me." I paused for a moment. My head started to hurt so I closed my eyes and just focused, remembering Dr. Powell's words, to focus on it, not fight it, to trust my friends. Images scrolled through my mind, memories. I opened my eyes and looked at Emily, who was obviously concerned with my state.

"I remember who Dr. Doom is."

"Great!" Emily shouted. "Now let's go." Emily stuffed her bag of apples and her book inside her backpack and followed me towards the parking lot.

Chapter 17

Secrets Revealed

We found Savannah alone by the bus stop. There was no one else around. I sat next to her on the bench as Emily stood just behind us keeping watch.

"Amelia, there's something I need to tell you, and something I need to show you," Savannah started saying. "Why is Emily here?" She started ringing her hands together.

"Don't worry. You can trust her." I grabbed Savannah's shoulder and gave her a comforting look. I needed her to trust us.

"Um, let's go to my house," Savannah said, once again tugging at her sleeve.

We got up and walked towards the waiting bus. Something wasn't right.

Once the city bus pulled up to Savannah's place we got out and walked the short block to her house. We stopped at the front door. Savannah looked at me for support, her eyes pleading. I nodded at her, hoping she wouldn't cry. I didn't know how to comfort her. I didn't even know what was bothering her. Was it the fact that she was going through with her plan? That she couldn't wait to see her father again? Was her own scheme making her nervous?

Savannah pulled a key from her pocket and unlocked the door. She pulled us inside and guided us down the hallway to the closed door where Emily and had I broken into Savannah's secret office, twice.

Savannah looked back at us, uncertain about what she was going to do. She pulled a pink key off a chain she was wearing around her neck. Unlocking the door, she turned off the laser system and beckoned us inside. She looked down the hallway before closing the door behind herself.

"I'm so sorry Amelia. I should have told you earlier. My uncle, he-"

I cut her off. "He did it. He put me in the hospital. I know."

Different images started flashing in my mind. I saw myself lying on the ground and Dr. Doom standing over me holding an odd weapon. I saw a lot of people walking around at a theme park. Then I was in an alley, and someone was turning the corner, coming right at me.

"I helped him do it!" Savannah practically shouted as tears started falling from her eyes, pulling me away from the images in my head. "I didn't know what he was planning. It's a sort of gun. I built it off a weapon design he had from the military. It harnesses waves of electricity and energy from the surrounding area. I wasn't finished with it

84

though. Uncle Jason took it out of here before I worked out the kinks."

That was why I didn't remember that Emily was my partner, or that Dr. Doom was Savannah's uncle. That was also why Savannah was acting so secretive and shy around me.

"Savannah, why are you telling me this?"

Savannah let her head droop as she closed her eyes. After a long, silent moment, she pulled up her shirt sleeve. A large bruise covered the upper part of her arm, followed by multiple scratches.

"What happened?"

Savannah wiped a tear from her face with her other arm. "I upset him. I wasn't working fast enough I guess."

"Your uncle did this?" I asked, looking back and forth between her bruised arm and her teary eyes. Savannah nodded her head.

"I can't handle it anymore. And it's too late for me to try and back out."

So, Savannah didn't want to do this. She was being forced to. No wonder Mrs. Bakers didn't want him in her home. Does she even know?

Savannah readjusted her shirt, covering up the dark bruises.

"Well if we're telling secrets," Emily began. "Amelia, Ms. Blanchard made me follow you."

Emily pulled my thoughts away from Savannah's beatings and onto her.

"It was you spying on me at headquarters?" I let a

85

small smile escape as I spoke.

"She told me she wanted someone to watch you. You don't turn in your reports until you have officially finished a case, but she told me to keep her updated on your progress."

"Why?"

"Wait, Ms. Blanchard?" Savannah asked. "I'm not sure I understand. Who's Ms. Blanchard?"

"Oops," Emily murmured.

I gave her a look as if to say 'Great'! Now I have to explain more.

"What are you talking about?" Savannah inquired, wiping her eyes.

I glared at Emily as I brought my hand up to my head as if I had a migraine. With a little more chaos, I just might. Emily just smiled her innocent smile at me. Should I tell Savannah about the T.S.O.? Would I get in trouble if I did? Probably.

"We're spies," Emily blurted out. She took a deep breath and then started to laugh. "Saying that was easier than I thought." Now I didn't have a choice.

"We work for a secret underground agency called the Teen Spy Organization." I explained. "We are both secret agents. And Emily shouldn't have such a big mouth."

Emily smiled at me while Savannah stood there staring at us with her mouth open. Even though I knew she was an agent now, I couldn't remember much about Emily or her connections to the T.S.O.

"Savannah, you can't tell anyone."

I looked around the room listening to the quiet hum

of all the different machines that surrounded us. These machines helped to produce the weapon that put me in the hospital and possibly caused this entire mess.

I glanced at the pin board above the two computer screens and I remembered Alexis asking about a red stone yesterday. Emily was giving her report to Ms. Blanchard and that must have been how Alexis found out about the stone.

"What is that rock called?" I asked Savannah pointing at the image on the wall.

"That's called a Bayshire stone. It's believed to have the ability to power an entire city, to manipulate the surrounding energy fields. It was recently found on an archeological dig. The investor has it in Ohio. My uncle wants to find it. He wants my help to find the stone and transfer its energy to some giant machine, a weapon that would make him capable of knocking out all power within half of the city. His goal is to knock out the power so he could make his way into the prison without being detected. All the security systems would be shut down."

Savannah looked up at the stone, then back at me. "Without the stone, he would have to find a way to knock out the systems from within the prison itself. I learned it was last transferred to a museum in Texas, on its way here. It's on tour. I'm not sure when it arrives. I can't even think about what would happen if my uncle actually got a hold of the stone. He might end up using it for more than just breaking my dad out of prison."

"This secret weapon he's working on puts everyone in danger," I said. I couldn't help but think there was still more to his plan. I had to tell Alexis about what I discovered.

Leaving Savannah's house, Emily and I walked outside. I was glad Savannah finally decided to open up to us. I can't believe Dr. Doom, Jason, had the nerve to hurt his own niece. The pain he inflicted was a lot worse than I thought.

"Bye Savannah," Emily said as we began walking down the sidewalk.

We made it two houses away. Savannah was still standing in her driveway. I looked back to wave at her, but her expressions alarmed me. "Run!" she shouted, waving her hands fanatically above her head. "Run! He's coming!"

Emily and I started running down the street and turned the corner. We crouched down between two trash cans. I watched as a small black car drove past us. Only half of the license plate was visible.

We waited until the car was around the corner and out of sight before coming out of our hiding place and made a run for it.

Once we were out of the neighborhood and away from danger, Emily and I slowed down. "I hope Savannah is going to be okay," I told Emily.

After walking for fifteen minutes my head started to ache. My muscles started to weigh down on me. Was I seriously this out of shape?

"Amelia," Emily started to say as we slowed down, "My mom never solved the case on Mr. Bakers."

"A few days ago," I looked over at Emily as I talked. "I looked into the T.S.O. files and found your mom's page. The file was empty." I ignored the pain in my head as we continued walking.

Emily and I walked on in silence. Turning the corner onto Emily's street, she stopped me. The pain got worse. My backpack became ten times heavier. Grabbing my arm,

Emily started shaking me, but I couldn't focus on what was going on. I felt dizzy. The sound of Emily's screaming voice started to fade.

My head was spinning. It felt like my brain was going to melt into water. I didn't think I could stand the pain much longer. I thought maybe Emily or her mom were calling me, but it was another memory.

I was back in the theme park, back in the alley with a phone held up to my ear. I listened to someone talk to me on the radio, and recognized the voice. It was Emily. A sense of relief came over me. I *knew* this was a memory, that this wasn't actually happening, I couldn't help but feel relieved.

"I found them. The agents are ready to transfer the information," Emily's voice said over the walkie talkie.

"Emily? I need help! Sending you my coordinates. Come quick! I have the information we need about Doom's identity, but there's too many of his henchman on my tail. They're waiting to see that I actually have the information before making any moves."

I could feel that fear inside the memory, the thumping in my chest. The relief of hearing Emily's voice was strong. People were tracking me, people who didn't want me sharing the newly found information. The amusement park wasn't safe anymore. My position was compromised. I had to get out.

Coughing I slowly got up. "Ag- Dr. Powell? What are you doing here?" There was a taste in my mouth, burning my tongue. The memory, the scene inside the theme park, was pulled away from me.

Looking around, Dr. Powell held a bottle of hot sauce in his hand. Emily breathed a sigh of relief.

"You fainted, again," Dr. Powell explained. Mrs. Steinfeld brushed a strand of hair out of my face as I sat up. I was on their living room couch.

"Amelia," Emily said, grabbing my attention, "I have to show you something. Come with me."

Now standing in the middle of Emily's room, as if I never fainted at all, she handed me a closed envelope. "It was on the front porch when we got home. I had to drag you here by the way."

I looked down at the envelope. Agent Z was written on the back. I looked up at Emily. "Open it," she encouraged.

Tearing open the letter, I pulled out a piece of folded paper and began reading.

Agent Z;

You need to stay away from Savannah. These are orders. She is working with someone, though I don't know who yet. Your mission is to stop both of them. I believe communicating with Savannah on a friendly level is just distracting you from finding out what she's really planning. I don't want you getting hurt.

Since you're staying with Emily, I suppose you might be able to put her help to good use, but just this once. For now, do not reveal your cover. You know the consequences.

-Ms. Blanchard.

Emily came up behind me. "What is it?" I handed

her the letter and she started reading.

I took a deep breath before saying anything to Emily. Ms. Blanchard really had me confused now. Why was she sending me letters? Why didn't she just call me into her office like she usually did? Or send a message through the T.S.O. system?

"Do you know why Ms. Blanchard is always on my back? We already know who Savannah is working with, her uncle. We already discovered what she's trying to hide from him, the Bayshire stone. The only consequences we might have are failing at this mission. For us to accomplish this mission we need to work together. Ms. Blanchard doesn't know what she's talking about. She has no idea what's really happening, and she doesn't need to know until I turn in my report. She has never been this involved with one of my cases."

Great. Now I'm questioning my supervisor. My fear finally broke through. I still couldn't remember everything. Could I even trust my own thinking? I didn't want to put anyone in danger. Or second guess the director of the T.S.O. Was that what Ms. Blanchard was getting at?

"You know what? This is our fight," I said to Emily.

No matter what it took, I couldn't let anyone get hurt. Not like I did.

Chapter 18

Saturday February 6th

Stolen Jewelry

After alerting the police of Dr. Doom's plan, Emily and I stood across the street from the city museum. I waited, watching intently with anticipation for something to happen.

The alarms started blaring and people rushed out the doors. The police cars were already parked outside. I tensed, preparing myself for the worst. Emily stood there in excitement, her ice cream starting to melt down the cone as she held it, not even aware of its presence.

Two police officers came walking out with Dr. Doom in handcuffs between them. Making their way down the front steps Dr. Doom managed to get his hands out of the cuffs. He punched one of the officer's in the face and pushed the other to the ground. I watched as Doom picked up a gleaming necklace from the ground near one of the officers.

Doom raced down the street, looking behind himself as he ran.

Emily and I began chasing after him. We ran down the opposite side of the street trying to catch up to Doom. I noticed he was running in the direction of the park. Emily threw the ice cream to the ground as we picked up speed.

"Hurry up Amelia, we're going to lose him!" Emily shouted from a few feet in front of me.

"Hey, I know a shortcut, this way!"

Emily followed me down a small road that led in between two buildings. As we rushed out the other side of the street the two of us tackled Doom. All three of us fell to the ground and the necklace flew out of Doom's pocket. Sirens could be heard in the distance as the police approached the scene. For a brief moment Emily lost her grasp, allowing Doom to move into a different position. I tried to hold onto him, to keep my grip. Emily tried to grab his coat. Doom kicked her in the knee and jabbed his elbow into her stomach. I lunged on top of him as Emily rolled over in pain. I looked over at her, distracted from the fight. Just as I turned back to Doom, he rolled over and grabbed me, throwing me off him.

Free from our grasp, Doom jumped to his feet and ran down the street. He didn't seem to notice he left the necklace.

A black car came screeching to a stop and Doom hopped into the passenger seat. The car sped down the street before I even made it to my feet.

"Come on!" I shouted in irritation. "We had him!" I stopped my foot on the ground, my blood boiling.

"It's alright. At least we got the necklace back," Emily said, holding her stomach as she got up and stood next to me. I wiped blood from my cheek, only then noticing it. There was also a scratch on my leg, but I was too focused on not catching Doom. I didn't even feel the pain.

Emily walked to where the necklace lay on the street, picked up the priceless jewelry and handed it to me. "Come on. Let's check in back at headquarters," she said.

Chapter 19

Someone on the Inside

Waking up in the middle of the night, I couldn't get myself to fall back asleep. We were lying on the floor in the living room. "Emily," I began whispering into the dark room. I started shaking her a little, grabbing her shoulders, trying to wake her up.

"What!" she said turning around, whispering back to me. She didn't sound too happy that I had woken her.

"Emily, I need answers. Right now. This isn't making sense and I can't sleep," I said.

"What are you talking about?"

"It doesn't make sense to me."

Emily got up out of the blankets and went into the kitchen. "This looks like it's going to be a long story. Better grab a snack." She pulled two cupcakes out of the fridge before walking back to me. "So, what's up?" Emily handed me a cupcake as she sat down on her blanket and took off the wrapper.

I thought about Savannah's dad, Mr. Bakers. It didn't seem like the case was handled properly to begin with.

"Well, your mom never closed the case about Savannah's dad. So why is he in jail then?" I asked. "Isn't it said that everyone in America is innocent until proven guilty?" Emily looked at me. I could tell she knew I was right. "Something's not right here," I continued trying to keep myself from shouting. "The T.S.O. cuffed him and dragged him away without completing a proper investigation. There has to be more to this story. I know it!"

"Amelia, calm down."

"I think your mom put Savannah's dad in jail without enough evidence. According to what little information there is available, they never proved he actually stole anything from the government."

"Okay, that's it," Emily exclaimed.

"What's 'it'?"

"Well," she pulled on her left shoe. "We are going down to headquarters, storming into Ms. Blanchard's office, and getting some answers. Ms. Blanchard is obviously hiding something." She put on the other shoe, ready for action.

"No! Ms. Blanchard can't know we're working together. Not yet. She doesn't want us to. She'll take us off the mission and assign someone else. We can't have that," I said.

"Your right," Emily responded. "Well, then we're going to have to do some research another way."

Emily grabbed my hand and guided me through the

kitchen. "We've got to go to the basement." I followed Emily with curiosity down the dark staircase to the basement. Why did she have a basement in California?

Once we reached the bottom, Emily turned on the lights. In the corner of the room was a workspace. A large desk backed up against the wall, files and papers thrown across the top, along with piles on the floor, leaning, ready to fall over without even a gust of wind.

"The desk is my mom's. That's where she works at home." Emily guided me through a door in the wall I hadn't previously noticed. There was another little room, with a desk, arm chair, coffee table, and slide-out storage bins. "And this is my office away from the office," Emily explained. "But you should already know that."

I was admiring the decorations she had on the wall. I loved all of the different colors and the abstract art she had hanging in every corner. Looking around the room, I had visions of Emily and I working in here. I remembered doing school work and attempting to crack cases.

Emily opened a drawer next to the desk and pulled out her laptop computer. After logging in, she entered her code for access to the T.S.O. files and database. "I don't see why they change the access code so much," Emily mumbled as she put in the code.

Once logged on, Emily opened a file called; *Recent cases for the T.S.O.*

In the search bar, she typed in Agent Steinfeld. The page took her from her personal information to her mom's.

Something clicked in my head. Mrs. Steinfeld was the bridge for the T.S.O. and the police. She took care of making sure the cover stories added up.

Emily ended up with the same page I did, with the

same missing information.

The only difference this time though, was that this is what it now stated:

My apologies, this case has not yet been added to the page. Someone has hacked into the T.S.O. system and this information is vital so it has been taken down until later notice. Thank you for your cooperation.

"Why did it tell you different information?" I wrinkled my brow. "Last time I opened up this page," I explained to Emily, "the information displayed here was different."

"Weird," Emily said, staring at the computer screen.

Who hacked the system?

"Let's just go back to bed." Emily sighed and turned off the computer. "We can look more tomorrow."

I didn't want to go back to sleep. I wanted answers, but Emily wasn't going to cooperate. Plus, I didn't even know what else I could do, not right now. There was no point in arguing about something I didn't completely understand.

Chapter 20

Don't Trust Anyone

The following morning, sitting at the counter in the Steinfeld's kitchen, Mrs. Steinfeld spoke to us about my parents' return.

Great! I kept thinking sarcastically as Mrs. Steinfeld told me that my parents' flight was landing tomorrow. That means that I had even less time in the field to do what needed to be done before my parents got home.

"Seriously?" I said before I realized how mean it sounded. "I mean, I love my parents with all my heart, but I wanted to finish this case before they came home, and to do that I can't be at the house."

"I know," Mrs. Steinfeld said with an understanding smile. "I just thought I should let you know. You've done well in the past. Why do you think it would be harder to do your job now? They're not even back yet. They're staying at a hotel tomorrow before driving home."

"I know, I'm just saying. Let's get some work done. We should spend as much time as possible trying to solve this case before they get back," I told Emily. She nodded in agreement. "We should start with the Bayshire Stone," I offered.

"Good idea," Emily said.

I grabbed my phone from my back pocket and Emily handed me a popsicle as we sat down on the front porch. I called Savannah, asking her to come over. We needed to talk.

About twenty minutes later she rode up and joined Emily and I on the porch. "What else is there Savannah? I know there's something you're not telling me," I started.

Before she answered, Emily handed her a popsicle. I thought Savannah was going to cry again. I hated seeing her like this. Something serious was bothering her, something at home.

"Savannah, what's wrong?" Emily asked seeing the same thing.

"Well, I- I'm not supposed to say," she said.

"Why not?" I said as calmly as I could without getting irritated.

"It's alright Savannah, it isn't your fault," Emily said trying to reassure her.

"But it is. I helped him and I'm still supposed to!" Savannah exclaimed.

"Don't trust anyone!" I heard Ms. Blanchard's voice ringing in my ear the first day of my training. I couldn't get her out of my head. I thought we could have trusted Savannah, but she's still working with Doom. I didn't trust Savannah's uncle when I first met him, but I never expected

him to be a criminal. Even Emily lied to me about our past. It was upsetting not knowing what was going on around me, what actually happened to me. I pushed the thoughts to the back of my mind. I had to focus on the here and now.

We sat in silence and finished the popsicles. Staring at the frozen treat an image came into my head. I was riding my bike with Emily, heading towards my neighborhood.

"We'll find Doom soon," Emily said. I nodded at her, wishing soon was now. It had been a few weeks since we stopped Doom from stealing the necklace at the museum, and there wasn't a single trace of his whereabouts. I was starting to think he left California, knowing I wouldn't be able to follow him out of the state. "Well," Emily continued. "I'll see you tomorrow at headquarters." Emily rode off and I turned the corner into my neighborhood. A few minutes later Doom showed up, leading to the need of a new bike tire and memory loss.

I looked up at Emily, wondering now if she blamed herself for my accident since she was the last person I was with. My memory was slowly coming back. A huge relief, but I still couldn't shake that feeling that I was in this alone.

"Amelia, come with me," Savannah said, pulling me back to present time. "I need you to come to my house. Something is happening tonight, and I want to talk about it there," she said.

"Very well. Let's go see what you have," I said. Hopefully I could figure out when Dr. Doom was planning his heist, when I could stop him.

Chapter 21
Tomorrow

Arriving at Savannah's house she warned us. "We have one hour till you guys need to leave. My mom works 'till eight, but my uncle will be back in about an hour."

She guided us to the back room. Once we were all settled in the room and the lasers were turned off, Savannah shut down the security cameras.

"Let's go over everything we know," Emily said.

"Dr. Doom is your uncle," I started, "and he wants to help Savannah's dad escape from jail."

"And he's forcing me to help him," added Savannah.

"And the Bayshire stone?" I asked.

"It is very powerful. Uncle Jason wants to use it to shut off all the power in the prison during his attack. That way the security system will be out of the way."

"What if he doesn't get the stone?" I asked, wondering if we could do something about that.

"He's planning to take the stone from the museum later today. If he can't get it easily, he has a plan to break in without it," Savannah explained. "He's taking just about every precaution possible. He doesn't want to get caught stealing something if he can work his way around it.

"What is his plan?" Emily asked.

"I'm not sure yet. That's what he's coming over later to discuss with me," Savannah said.

"Is he working with anyone else?" I asked.

"Anyone besides me? I don't think so."

"Well, we need to find the stone before Dr. Doom." I looked back and forth between the two girls as I spoke. "I have an idea who can help us. If we can't get it though, you've got to get those other plans to us as soon as possible."

"Okay," Savannah said.

"What was it you wanted to share with us anyways?" Emily asked.

"Oh," Savannah started. "He's planning on breaking in to the prison tomorrow night at six, just after visiting hours are over."

"Tomorrow?" How could Savannah not have shared this before?

"Yes."

I looked at Emily with urgency. "We have to get that stone," I said. "Now."

Chapter 22

The Bayshire Stone

Emily and I walked into T.S.O. headquarters. "I didn't even know Alexis was here," Emily whispered into my ear as we made our way through the different halls. We kept our heads down, avoiding Ms. Blanchard's office, hoping not to run into her. I knew it was risky being caught with Emily here, but I didn't have any other choice.

We walked into the cafeteria, finding Alexis sitting at a table in the middle of the room. Emily waved as Alexis looked up at us from her phone. "We need to talk," I said as Emily and I sat down across from her.

"What is it? Why are you whispering?" Alexis whispered back as she leaned across the table.

"We need your help," Emily said. "We don't want Ms. Blanchard knowing. By the way it's nice to see you," Emily added.

"You said you were here on business. You were

looking for some type of stone. The Bayshire?" I asked.

"That's right. And I know exactly where it is," Alexis said. She had a huge smile on her face. "I discovered the stone is owned by a private investor who collects rare objects from both earth and space. The Bayshire is currently on tour and going on exhibit here at the Glayfield Earth and Space Museum. I was going to retrieve it tonight."

"We have to go after it now," I said, "as in right now."

"Why?" Alexis asked.

"Dr. Doom, the guy we're tracking down, is planning on stealing it within the next few hours. We can't let that happen," Emily said. Alexis's face showed what we were all feeling.

Thirty minutes later, the three of us walked into the Glayfield Earth and Space Museum. Alexis explained that the stone was in the underground storage area waiting to be put on exhibit tomorrow.

As we walked through the museum Alexis never stopped scanning the area for threats. I could tell she was on guard, but I couldn't figure out why she was so nervous. We got on one of the elevators and Alexis took us to the basement level, two floors underground. We walked down the hall and approached a door that read; **Authorized Personnel Only.** Alexis grabbed the door knob and rushed us inside, shutting the door behind us. Alexis pulled out a key card.

"The stone is in storage locker D32," Alexis said. "It will probably be in a black case with a four-digit code and a key." Alexis handed me a decoding device from the small bag she was carrying. Emily placed it inside her backpack. "Your key card should work just fine for the other part. I'll guard the door," Alexis said.

"Thanks," I nodded at her. Alexis closed the door, standing guard on the other side.

We stopped and looked at the map taped on the inside of the door. I was glad for the map and clearly posted signs at the end of the aisles. There seemed to be an endless number of aisles and walkways marked with letter and number combinations. I looked at the halls in front of us, one to the left, one to the right, and one right down the middle. Each row contained countless rooms probably filled with lockers and safes of every size. Finding where we were on the map, I quickly found an aisle marked with the letter D sectioning off from the hallway to our right. We didn't have to walk too far before we came across the hallway marked with the letter D. We headed down the aisle to find a door marked with the number "32".

"You have your key card, right?" I asked Emily.

"Yeah." I pulled out my key card and unlocked the door, planning to use Emily's for the briefcase Alexis told us about.

Inside the dimly lit room was an empty display case, waiting to be used. On the other side of the space there was a table full of black cases.

"Which one is it?" Emily asked.

"I'm not sure." I picked up one case. Emily did the same. Looking at it I found an item number on the case. It didn't say anything else about what was inside though. I looked at the lock to find only a key insert.

"It could be this one," Emily offered. The case she held had both a key and a code lock. I picked up the last case on the table to find both types of locks as well.

106

"We only have one shot with the key card," I said. Emily took a deep breath.

"What if Alexis was wrong and it's only a key lock?" Emily asked.

"We can't take that chance."

"Well, then which one do we choose?"

"I don't know," I said, shaking my head. I didn't think it would be this hard. "You pick."

Emily took out the decoder device and the key card from her bag. Taking the case in her hand she attached the decoding device and went to work. I watched her with anticipation, my heart racing. I heard the faint click of the lock and a small bit of anxiety left me. "Here goes nothing," Emily said. I held my breath. Emily scanned the lock with her card and slowly unlocked the case.

Emily looked at me. I kept quiet, hoping we picked the right one. She loosened her grip around the handle and opened it. Inside was a red stone. I sighed with relief. Emily let out a small laugh.

Emily took it out of the case and put it in her "backpack of everything." Closing the case, we left the room and hurried back down the way we came. I saw security cameras hidden in the corners of the ceilings as we ran past. The T.S.O. would have to help wipe those.

"Did you get it?" Alexis asked as we opened the door.

"It's in the bag," Emily said, nodding her head towards her backpack.

"Alright," Alexis started. "Let's get out of here." Alexis looked behind her uneasily as we made our way to the entrance of the museum. He hair was tousled and out of place.

"You okay?" I asked.

"Just peachy," Alexis responded, smiling at me.

As we were about to leave the lobby, Alexis, turned abruptly by the exit. "What is it?" I asked.

"Nothing," Alexis said. Her eyes were wary as she gave me a not-so-encouraging smile. Why was her hair so messed up? "Let's get out of here," she said, turning and walking out the door, Emily and I following behind.

Alexis took the stone, agreeing to take it into headquarters instead of Emily and me chancing Ms. Blanchard spotting us. "Doom will never find it there," Emily said as she handed Alexis the backpack in the parking lot.

"I agree," I said, knowing the Bayshire would be safe inside headquarters.

After Alexis left, Emily and I walked over to our bikes. Before getting on my bike, a young man bumped into my shoulder. "Hey," I said, turning and looking over at him. He turned to face me, but didn't say anything. He had buzz cut hair, and dark brown eyes, but showed no sign of an apology. He glared at me, anger seeping out of his eyes before he turned away, continuing down the street.

We headed off, riding down the street towards Emily's house.

As we arrived at Emily's, Savannah called me. I walked back and forth in Emily's room, listening intently to every word Savannah said. "Alright," I said. "I'll see you then. Thanks."

"What is it?" Emily asked, sitting patiently on the edge of her bed.

"Savannah just told me about her uncle's plan. She emailed you the information. We've got to get ready."

Chapter 23

Preparations

Emily and I spent the next morning packing everything we might need into her "backpack of everything". We included a grappling hook pen, though I doubt we would need it, my key card, and night vision goggles. I didn't sleep the night before. I was up worrying about the plan, about everything that could go wrong, but I was fully awake.

We printed out the blueprints and plans from Emily's computer, found the various bus routes, and determined which one we needed to be on.

"Wow!" Emily said as she began reading Dr. Dooms notes. "He has this whole thing mapped out; a way to get past the guards, the blueprints for the prison and the directions to the control room, doors, gates, vents, and alarms. This guy is ready for anything."

"Except us," I said as I looked at the blueprints with Emily. "He wants to get into the control room to shut off the security cameras. It looks like the next thing he does is knock out the guards in the hallway that leads to the different cells and facilities. Look, he even has an X on a certain cell."

"But what about this? He has a circle five cells down from that. I think we're missing something here," Emily said. "Do you see these little dots that he put in the hallway? Those must be the guards. They don't want anyone getting in there."

"Dr. Doom is a lot smarter than he sounds," I said.

"Yeah, well he isn't that smart when it comes to picking a code name." Emily started laughing at her own joke. I couldn't help but laugh along with her.

"We should see if Alexis can help us," I said.

"Good idea. I'll give her a call," Emily said. She picked up her phone and left the room. I picked up the blueprints and stuffed them in her backpack. Taking a pair of night vision goggles I strapped them to my belt.

The timer on my watch chimed just as Emily walked into the room. It was time to go. As we walked to the front door my stomach turned with excitement. We grabbed our bikes and were ready to go just as Alexis pulled up in the driveway using a bike from the T.S.O. We had half an hour before we had to be on the bus and a twenty-minute bike ride to the bus stop.

Chapter 24
Closing Time

We stopped at a little ice cream parlor near the bus stop. Once we all got our ice cream, we settled down at the last available table in the very back of the parlor. We went over everything again with Alexis.

Not looking up from the blueprints laid out across the table, Emily explained. "Thanks to Savannah, we have all the plans and information we need. Dr. Doom is going to arrive there at six o'clock. Once he gets there, he's going to leave Savannah in the van to monitor his steps and help him locate all the guards. She's going to come and meet us instead."

"As soon as the last group of people leave," I started, "he's going right through the front door, straight to the electrical room, to knock out the power. After that, he heads to the prison cells." I pointed to the blueprints on the table, directing Alexis to the location Doom would go to. "We're assuming this cell here is where Mr. Bakers is." I pointed to the cell block with the X on it.

"What about this one?" Alexis asked, pointing to the cell that was circled.

"I'm not sure. It's in a completely different part of the building. I'm just hoping we're going to the right place. We've got to stop him there, before he opens the cell."

Once the time hit five-thirty we packed up the blueprints. We walked outside to the bus stop and got on the next bus, bringing our bikes with us. The bus ride only took ten minutes. After getting off the bus, it was ten more minutes on our bikes to get to the prison gates. By the time the three of us arrived at the prison's outer gate, we had five minutes until Dr. Doom and Savannah arrived.

There was a large fence around the facility with barbed wires on the top. The only way in was through the front gate that would only open from the control panel inside the guard tower.

"Should we use the grappling hook?" Emily asked as she peered up at the top of the fence.

"No need," Alexis said. Turning towards her I saw what she was looking at. A small group of visitors, led by two guards, was heading towards the slowly opening gate. The three of us ran to join the group and walked in without being noticed.

After walking inside, we went to the front office and sat in the waiting room. In the room was a lady that looked to be in her mid-twenties. There was also a little girl and her dad and a guy signing papers at the front desk. Behind the desk was a tall man wearing a guard's uniform.

We sat and joined the group, keeping to ourselves. A while later, the group of visitors gathered and began to walk out. The prison's visiting hours were now ending. We followed behind the group and walked outside.

We parted away from the group of visitors and slid around the corner of the building, hiding behind a row of bushes. We only had to wait a few moments before we saw a tall figure approaching the building on foot. He was across the parking lot walking from the direction of the front gate. As he got closer, I recognized Dr. Doom. His features weren't clear because of how far away he was, but as he pulled a black ski mask from his jacket pocket and slipped it over his head I was sure it was him. We watched Savannah's uncle as he approached the front door.

I crouched lower between the bushes, not wanting to be seen. My heart was racing with anticipation. Dr. Doom pulled a gun from the insides of his coat, aimed at the door, and pulled the trigger. The door burst inward. After the dust cleared, Doom was gone from my view, already inside the building. My heart started beating faster.

After Doom disappeared inside the building, Emily, Alexis, and I raced to the front gate. We discovered the guards at the gate shack weren't there. I looked around the control panel and found the button that controlled the front gate. Opening it up, Savannah made her way through and met us inside the guard shack.

Chapter 25

The Take Down

"How did your uncle get in?" Alexis asked as we closed the gate from inside the shack.

"He had a fake prison ID and tricked the guard into opening the gate. Once he was inside, he took them out using knock out darts. The guards aren't dead, but they're unconscious."

"I hate violence," Emily said.

"Then why did you become an agent? You should know by now that it comes with the territory," Alexis commented.

"Well at least he made it easier for us to get in," I said. "Where are the guards anyway?"

Emily walked all the way around the guard post. We waited by the opened door, right up next to the closed gate. After a couple minutes, she appeared in the doorway.

"They're lying against the gate on the other side, up against the post's wall."

"That sounds comfortable," Alexis said, attempting to lighten the mood.

"Come on, we need to hurry," I said as I refocused my thoughts on the task at hand.

"Wait a moment," Alexis said. "If you're not in the truck, won't Doom realize that?" she asked Savannah.

"Yeah," Emily said, crossing her arms. Anger rushed through me, but just for a second. Was Savannah still working for her uncle? Was this all a trick?

"He was just going to have me give him directions through the prison since the lights were going to be off. I made a recording. It's playing into his earpiece.

I nodded. Smart. If I knew this beforehand, we could have given him wrong directions. Too late for that now though.

We rushed back to the main visitor's entrance for the prison. I couldn't wait to catch Doom.

I looked through the now empty doorway and saw the guard at the front desk. He was lying on the floor, his hand cuffed to the bottom of the desk. I stepped over the shattered pieces of glass and broken wood from the door, rushing over to the guard.

"Hey," I said, shaking his shoulders, "Are you okay?" Slowly the guard opened his eyes and looked up at me. There was one door on each side of the desk in the office. "Where do the doors lead?" I asked as I uncuffed the guard, using a key Alexis found inside the desk.

Doom's plan was to go to the control room and turn off all the security cameras. Hopefully we could stop him there.

"Who are you kids?" the man asked as he sat up on the floor, rubbing his wrists.

"Special agents of the T.S.O. How do I get to the electrical room?"

Still in a daze the guard stood up from the floor and leaned over his computer, opening up the security system.

"There is no point in going through the door that says 'cells' on it," the guard said. "It's a false sign designed to confuse intruders. It just leads outside to a storage area. It's silly really. The other door leads to the electrical control room." The guard looked up at us in confusion. "What's the T.S.O.?"

I watched the figure of Dr. Doom on the monitors, ignoring the guard's question. He was moving through the control room. He began messing with the video system switch board.

The computer screens all turned to static. Doom must have turned off the cameras.

"I can explain later," I told the guard. "Right now, we need your help. That guy on the camera is trying to break someone out of your prison." After a moment of contemplation, the guard, gestured for us to follow him.

Stopping in front of the door to the 'Electrical Control Room', The guard opened the door and we all entered together.

We saw Dr. Doom working at a computer terminal near the far wall. He was wearing his signature ski mask.

"Put your hands on your head!" The guard ran to Doom, pinning him against the desk and forcing his hands behind his back. I held my breath as the guard slapped handcuffs on both of Doom's wrists. "You have the right to remain silent. Anything you say can and will be used against you," the guard said.

That was a lot easier than I thought it would be. I let out a sigh of relief as Emily put her hand on my shoulder. Part of me was jealous. I wanted to be the one to say that, to cuff Doom and drag him away.

I went over to Doom and pulled off the mask. Dropping it to the floor, my heart sank as a chill ran down my spine.

It wasn't Dr. Doom, but an accomplice throwing us off his trail. His henchman started laughing sarcastically, believing he had helped Doom beat us.

"I thought he was here!" Savannah exclaimed. She threw her hands in the air in confusion.

"He knew the guard would check the control room so he sent someone else to do that part." I said, tightening my grip on the man's shoulder. "I should have known he wouldn't just walk in here!" I said. He even gave Savannah incorrect notes, as if he knew she was working with us, to throw her off the trail.

"I know you!" Alexis exclaimed. "I saw you when I first arrived at headquarters! On the subway." Alexis glared at him. "You're a new computer technician. You just joined the T.S.O. I should have known something was up when I first met you." The man smiled a crooked smile, letting out another horrid laugh between his toothy grin.

"Do you act alone within the T.S.O.?" Emily asked.

The man laughed. "I get my orders from someone deep within the T.S.O." He smiled ruefully.

"Who is it?" I shouted, grabbing his arm and twisting

118

painfully. I needed to know what he was talking about. The thought of someone working inside the T.S.O. made me shiver with anger and betrayal. How could I not have seen this coming?

"You will never find out Agent Z. My loyalty goes far beyond Dr. Doom." He continued to laugh hysterically, throwing his head back with a sneer.

I pushed the man toward the security guard. "He's all yours."

It all made sense now. He was the one who hacked the T.S.O.'s system, along with erasing the files about Doom on Mrs. Steinfeld's computer.

"Come on, I think I know where he is," I said running out the door, the others not far behind me. The guard stayed behind, taking care of Doom's crooked double agent. Thanks to the blueprints, I knew which building Mr. Bakers was being held in, and which cell.

We ran outside, heading for the prison quarters on the blueprints. It was dark outside now as I lead the others across the complex towards building D. Remembering all of the markings on Doom's map of the prison, I was sure he would be heading in that direction. As we approached building D, I noticed a side door was left open. We ran towards it, slowing down as we approached.

I couldn't see a thing inside the building, my vision being enveloped in darkness. We stood, not breathing. My eyes adjusted to the darkness. Shadows were moving around in the hallway. I could feel the others behind me, waiting for me to make a move. The sound of a thud came from somewhere down the hall, but I couldn't see that far ahead. It sounded like someone falling to the floor. Uh-oh.

Chapter 26

Through the Cell Block

I moved down the hall with my team right behind me, taking one step at a time. I took another step forward. Something hit my foot. My heart skipped a beat as I froze. Peering down, a man was lying on the ground, my foot touching his pant leg. I looked at the man on the floor. He was dressed in a guard uniform, unconscious.

"Stay close," I hushed under my breath, turning around towards Emily and Alexis even though I couldn't see them. I looked ahead of me, wishing I could see the enemy.

I remembered my tool belt and grabbed a pair of goggles from the pouch. I put them up to my face and peered further down the hall. Through the night vision goggles I could see Doom about twenty feet down the hall in front of us. He was leaning over another guard, passed out on the ground. He was searching the man's pockets.

I turned around to see Alexis and Emily both wearing their night vision goggles. Signaling to Emily, we both ran for Doom. I couldn't wait to get my hands on him.

Just as he managed to retrieve something from the guard's pocket, he stood up and looked in our direction. He must have seen us because he ran in the opposite direction down the hall. Gaining speed Emily and I chased him down the hallway to the center of the building.

As we closed the distance on Dr. Doom, I rushed past Emily and collided into the man, knocking him over a desk. I pulled at his shirt collar, preventing him from getting up. "This is wrong Doom!" I shouted at him.

He grabbed my arm and twisted it, releasing my grip on his shirt. At that time the building began to get louder. Inmates began shouting at us from behind their cell doors. I looked around for a moment, confused from all the shouting. Dr. Doom pushed me off of him.

Turning away from the table, I reached for Doom. My shoe was snagged on the table leg. "Are you kidding me?" Turning back to the table I managed to release my foot from its grasp. Doom made his way down another hallway.

Through my night vision goggles I saw Emily run past me, chasing him down the corridor. I ran after them. Emily and I ran side by side now, only a few feet between us and Doom. I could hear footsteps behind us, probably Savannah and Alexis. I focused on Doom in front of me, Emily beside me, and pushed myself to run harder. As we approached another corridor, we tackled him to the floor, the two of us trying to restrain him from getting away. He kicked at us, yelling. "You can't stop me!"

"We'll see about that," I replied. Doom punched Emily in the face, knocking her off his chest. Adrenaline racing through my body, I punched Doom in the nose.

The darkness around us began to fade. The color in my goggles changed and I noticed the lights in the room beginning to flicker. The guard we left behind must have managed to get the electricity working again. I took off my goggles and threw them behind me.

Doom kicked at me. I rolled off him, landing beside him on my back. Doom got up and tried to escape back down the hall. Just as he made it to his feet, I swept my leg around and knocked him off balance. His feet came out from under him, and he crashed on the floor in front of me. I got to my feet and turned to face him. Sitting up now, he pulled an odd looking gun out of his coat pocket. The weapon looked familiar. He aimed the gun at my face and I froze. Fear filled my thoughts as I recognized the weapon as the one that put me in the hospital. It had to be.

Before he could pull the trigger, Emily kicked him in the wrist, sending the weapon flying into the air. "Never bring a weapon into a prison," she said, wiping blood from her lip. I quickly swung my leg, kicking him in the chest. As the air escaped his lungs Doom fell back to the floor.

Savannah and Alexis came running up behind us. Doom's eyes opened wide in astonishment at the sight of Savannah, then back to frustration, as he realized he was played.

Alexis didn't hesitate to jump down on top of Dr. Doom as she ran towards us. Emily and I each grabbed his arms. His kicking and bucking were not enough to escape. With a twist of his arms, we managed to lift Doom just enough to roll him onto his stomach. As Emily and I held his arms securely behind his back, Alexis was able to get a pair of handcuffs onto Doom's wrists.

"There's no point in struggling," I said as he continued to resist. "What's this?" I asked, grabbing a pair of keys from his pocket. "Ahh, this is what you took from that guard. Nice try."

With him lying on the floor Alexis sat on top of him, preventing him from putting up any more of a fight.

At the end of the hall the door quickly opened. A group of guards burst into the hallway running in our direction. "Quiet down!" one of them shouted as the group rushed towards us.

It wasn't until that moment that I realized how loud it had become with all of the inmates yelling from inside their cells and banging on the doors. Had Dr. Doom managed to open the cell doors, it would have been an all-out riot. Seeing the guards entering the area however, the inmates began to take the level of shouting down to a whisper.

"The name's Captain Willison," one of the men said. He wore the same uniform as everyone else. He had a square face, the lines indicating that he smiled a lot. Captain Willison put his hand out for me to shake. His expression showed obvious confusion at the scene that was taking place in front of him. Four teens in his prison, a full-grown man pinned on the floor, and night vision goggles lying in the middle of the hall. I smiled. We probably weren't what he was expecting to find on his way over here.

"Agent Z of the T.S.O.," I replied as I shook his hand. His grip was firm and controlling. "This is Mr. Jason. He likes to call himself Dr. Doom though." I gestured towards our suspect.

"Doom? Well," Captain Willison started with a laugh, "we'll take it from here."

"Thank you, sir. I would like to have a few words with him first though." I turned to Doom, smiling ear to ear. "Well, Doom, it seems like we did stop you. It seems appropriate that it all ends here. It looks like you're going to be here for a long time." Doom glared at me as I said goodbye and turned away from him. I couldn't get the smile on my face to leave. It felt so good to actually have caught Dr. Doom.

Dr. Doom caused a lot of problems for me and others. I was glad to put him behind bars.

I picked up the gun from the floor and inspected it carefully, turning it over and over in my hands. It was the same weapon he used to put me in the hospital before any of this started, when I first lost my memory. I could see it clearly in my head now. It seemed so long ago that it happened.

I pulled the prison blueprints out of Emily's backpack. Opening them up I located the markings that resembled where Savannah's father must be located. Walking over to one of the guards, I asked him to show me to the cell which was marked on the map.

Savannah walked next to me as we followed the guard down another long corridor. "It's that one right there." The man pointed towards a cell on the left side of the wall. As Savannah and I peered through the door, I saw one man sitting at the edge of a bed. He leaned over, his shoulders hunched. His hands wrung themselves together, over and over again. He was anxious. As he looked up at us, his expression seemed to change from excitement to anger. Savannah's face went pale.

I studied the man carefully, trying to match his face with the image of his mug shot I saw a while ago. His hair wasn't the right color. It was brown instead of black. His eyes had the look of bloodlust. Savannah leaned over to me, talking into my ear. "That's not my dad."

"What do you mean?" I asked as we turned away from the man in the cell. I could tell it was a different man, but I didn't want to believe it. It had to be him.

"That's Mr. Kathman, my uncle's old partner." I looked at her in amazement, my shock turning into understanding. Doom never wanted Mr. Bakers out of prison. He was here to break out his partner. He had fooled everyone, even Savannah. He probably even framed his brother. I couldn't help but feel sorry for her. I squeezed my hands into fists, trying to keep my anger under control. How could I have not seen this coming?

I grabbed Savannah by the shoulders and pulled her into a hug. "Are you okay?" I asked. Her eyes glossed over. She was trying to hold back tears. Savannah nodded in reply.

As we made our way back to the others, I noticed Dr. Doom standing up now. The captain of the guards was standing behind him holding on to his arm. I walked up to Dr. Doom and slapped him across the face. His surprise was priceless. The slight burning sensation in my hand was comforting. Doom looked at me with nothing but anger. Let him. He can't hurt me anymore.

The captain pulled Dr. Doom back with one hand and held the other out towards me, preventing any further aggression.

"Do you understand what you put your niece through?" I asked Doom. Everyone waited for an explanation from him, but none came.

"We explained everything to the captain," Alexis told me, wanting to calm me down. I ignored her efforts.

"He lied to Savannah," I started. I wanted to scream, but kept my voice just below a shouting level. "He was never here for her dad. He was here to break out Mr. Kathman, his old partner. He probably even framed Mr. Bakers as well."

The look Doom had on his face told me I was right. Emily looked at me, her brow wrinkled. She put her hand on my shoulder. I took a deep breath, clenching my fists. I wanted to hit him again.

"We will definitely look into it Agent Z," Captain Willison assured me.

Chapter 27
Aftermath

Leaving the prison and getting onto our bikes, we headed home.

"Amelia, there is still one thing I don't quite understand," Emily started. "I overheard Ms. Blanchard telling you they caught the guy you were fighting, who put you in the hospital. Since it wasn't Dr. Doom but Mr. Kathman, why did she lie?"

"I'm not sure. Maybe she thought it was him. At the time I was the only one who knew of his identity. She has definitely been acting a little strange lately. We'll have to look into that later," I replied.

Savannah didn't get to see her dad, but her uncle was getting what he deserved. Hopefully her dad would be going home soon. I could only hope the best, that if Mr. Bakers was innocent, his name would be cleared. Savannah insisted on talking to her mom about everything on her own. I agreed. She deserved to know, and it would be better coming from her own daughter.

Mrs. Steinfeld let Alexis spend the night at Emily's house. The three of us immediately fell asleep. Parts of the day continuously played themselves in my head. Meeting at the ice cream shop, finding the double agent in the electrical room, walking around in the dark inside the prison, piling on top of Doom, and watching his anger bubble as we arrested him.

Upon waking up the following morning I had a conversation with Mrs. Steinfeld; after all, Mr. Bakers' case was technically assigned to her.

I went over all the events of the night before. I explained to her that I believed Mr. Bakers was framed by Dr. Doom. After laying out all the details she agreed to reopen the case and reevaluate everything. There was no way that Savannah's dad could have done any of the crimes he was said to have committed. Doom on the other hand, was more than capable of stealing government information.

Chapter 28

New Assignment

An hour after my conversation with Mrs. Steinfeld there was a knock at the front door.

"We missed you so much, Amelia, we're so glad you're alright," Mom said to me as she wrapped her arms around me in a hug. I let her love envelop me and her hair cover my face. I would never be able to tell her about the T.S.O. It would take that genuine smile and throw it away. She would never trust me again.

My parents never liked to leave me for more than a week at a time. In a way, that was a good thing. I liked that they cared. If my parents knew what I spent my time doing I would be grounded till high school graduation.

Once I was packed, my parents loaded everything into the car and headed home.

I walked into my room and placed my backpack on

my bed. My phone began ringing. I took it out of my pocket and answered the unknown number, wondering who would be calling.

"Amelia? It's Alexis. I wanted you to know that I'm heading back to Ohio. The Bayshire stone is safe in my care and it looks like your job is done too," Alexis said. Part of her sounded uneasy.

"Thanks Alexis. Your help was greatly appreciated. Will I be seeing you anytime soon?" I asked, not mentioning how nervous she sounded over the phone.

"Afraid not."

"Well, you take care of yourself then." I put the phone down on the bed, and leaned down into my pillow. The exhaustion was getting to me. I was glad the case was over, that Doom couldn't hurt any more people like he had hurt Savannah and me.

Later that night my phone started ringing as I was unpacking my bag. "Agent Z, we are needed at the office ASAP." I recognized Emily's voice even though she didn't identify herself. For her to call me professionally and not even wait for my response meant something important. I needed to get to headquarters.

Persuading my parents that I left something important at Emily's and that I couldn't wait until morning, I made my way out of the house and to my secret entrance to the Teen Spy Organization.

Walking into the alley, I found the secret entrance to the T.S.O. headquarters hidden in the brick wall. The sensor scanned my hand, and I stepped onto the cement block that opened up to the elevator. Whoosh. I went down the tube-like elevator, and landed right at the entrance of the Teen

Spy Organization headquarters.

The same receptionist that's always been there smiled at me. This time I knew who she was. She must have been the one that called 911 on the day of my accident. I remembered passing her on my way home. I silently thanked her, knowing it could have been a lot worse without her.

Instead of walking straight to the doors, I stopped in front of them. "Thank you," I said, looking right at the woman.

"Just doing my job Agent Z." I nodded at her and watched as she pushed the button hidden on her desk that opened the double doors.

Walking into Ms. Blanchard's office, I found Emily and Savannah.

"What is this?" I asked, confused about why Savannah was there.

"Agent Z, you have a new mission." What was it? I didn't even turn in my report yet. After all, we only stopped Doom not even twenty-four hours ago. Not to mention the fact that Emily was here, who I wasn't even supposed to remember worked here, and Savannah, who shouldn't even know the Teen Spy Organization existed.

"We believe Doom had possession of classified government information. You and your team are to find out what exactly he knew and where he got this information. It's very important we don't have any more people working on the inside. That can't happen again," Ms. Blanchard said. Her usual straight face made me shiver. How did she even know this? No. I couldn't question Ms. Blanchard. That wasn't my job.

"Yes Ma'am." If I asked her how she knew what happened, she would have gotten upset. I couldn't question her authority.

I thought about the odd letter she sent me, how she told me to stay away from Savannah. She had never done something like that before. Not that I could remember. Of course, my memory wasn't very trustworthy at the moment.

"You are also going to train Savannah on the way. She is now being recruited by the organization." Savannah? An agent? She was a great scientist and engineer, sure. But she didn't seem like the usual T.S.O. agent. I kept my thoughts to myself.

"Savannah," Ms. Blanchard directed her attention towards her. "Because of your scientific knowledge I think you would be a great asset to the T.S.O., if you accept."

"I accept," Savannah said, smiling from ear to ear. I pushed the uneasy feeling to the bottom of my stomach, plastering a smile on my face.

I still found it interesting that Savannah wouldn't be sent to the training camp like every other agent. That's how all the teens started out, where we got our first taste of being on the job. Every teen to be recruited had to spend at least one year at the training camp to see if they had what it takes. Then they went to advanced training. Ms. Blanchard was losing her toughness.

We left Ms. Blanchard's office as she guided us through the facility. I couldn't tell if Emily noticed the same things about Ms. Blanchard that I did. Ms. Blanchard guided us into the office Emily and I would now be sharing. Emily immediately went to a rolling chair and sank right into it, the wheels sliding back a few feet in sync with her heavy sigh.

"Good luck agents," Ms. Blanchard said. She turned and left us without another word.

"So, I get to be an agent?" Savannah asked, soaking everything in.

"Only if you want to of course," I replied. "You have to put in the effort and the time. It isn't a walk in the park." I didn't mean to sound so strict, but the words were uttered before I could stop it. Ms. Blanchard was still on my mind. Maybe I was even jealous about how Savannah was being treated.

"Yes ma'am," Savannah said with a smile.

This was going to work out just fine. I would make sure of that. Savannah was going to be a good agent under my training. The uneasy feeling slowly left as I looked around the office. It was bigger than my old one. Better. Our new combined desk space was much bigger than what we each had separately. There were two boxes on the desk. One holding my stuff, the other holding Emily's. They already moved our belongings. There was a white board hanging on the wall and a banner with the T.S.O. sign on it. It was perfect.

I judged we had completed our last simple mission. If simple was even a word in the T.S.O.'s vocabulary. By the look of our new office, we were being moved up a level. I felt calm now, leaving the odd behavior of Ms. Blanchard to be handled another day.

"Check out this office," Emily said. She turned around in the chair, staring up at the ceiling.

"Alright," I started, looking between Emily and Savannah. We had a lot to get done. "Let's get to work."

Acknowledgments

A big thank you to my parents for their dedicated support and encouragement to pursure my dreams, and to Chelsea Fuchs, whose knowledge and guidance helped bring this story to life.

About the Author

R.E. Klinzing lives with her family in Southern California. She enjoys reading, playing volleyball, ASL, and playing guitar when she isn't writing stories filled with adventure and mystery. Finding Doom is the first in a series of crime adventures facing the agents of the T.S.O. It's the author's goal to have a positive impact on the world and those she reaches through her writing.

Made in the USA
San Bernardino, CA
03 December 2019